i

Man in the Bath

By Kit Derrick

ISBN 978-1-8384267-3-6

2nd edition

https://www.facebook.com/Hypnopub

Contents

Not all superheroes wear masks. But many of them do. To protect their secret identities and allow them to go about their business saving the world, safe from evil, and autograph hunters. And that was always in my mind at the very beginning. I didn't want the plaudits or the acclaim from the public, I just wanted to do good.

By now quite a lot of you have asked me individually for my story, so here it is, the relevant bits anyway, just a brief history of 'The Man in the Bath.' Very short, but as it has been frequently requested, and to save me from answering the same questions over and over again. That would leave me no time for my real work, paid or otherwise.

Well, to start at the beginning (as they say) I'm just a normal guy, nothing special. And in the very beginning, where we're starting, I never imagined that I would be responsible for anything this big or this important. Honestly, I didn't! But it turns out that I'm not alone in my thinking; that we are not alone, that there are a lot of similar people out here in cyberspace and in the flesh world too. Normal people. Normal people who have a moral sense and intelligence beyond the masses of sheep that populate our shops and schools, and councils and offices. It is just that we manage to hide our intelligence most of the time.

As you know, my friends, sometimes life is easier if you don't reveal your greater knowledge and wisdom. Other people don't like knowing that they're thicker than you are. Which means hiding your own intelligence. This, in itself, is ridiculous when you come to really think about it. And that was the reason I first started creating my little corner of the internet. I wanted to speak out. Educate. Share. Unafraid of my intelligence. In my normal, natural, speaking voice.

Now, I don't know where or when you choose to actively think about stuff (I've agonized over the best word to use here, as is my wont, but 'stuff' seems to be the best catch-all term), and, for me, the moments of clarity occur most frequently when I'm in the bath. Genuinely! At that wonderful, soaking moment when you're fully relaxed, the water is still piping hot, the bubbles are there (yes, I use Radox, and yes, I am secure enough in my own masculinity to admit I love the feel and comfort of bubble bath). And at that moment, I let my mind wander off to whatever flights of fancy drift into my conscious thoughts. I ponder 'stuff,' and deconstruct all sorts of random questions. I formulate and refine ideas.

Initially, I started to jot my thoughts down straight away when I got out of the bath, wrapped in a towel, and dripping onto the kitchen carpet. But that was quite unsatisfactory, as I'm sure you can imagine.

Next, I tried to take a paper and pen into the bath with me, but you just can't get comfortable like that, it feels contrived, is awkward, and anyway, it's impossible to relax fully when you're constantly worried about dropping soluble items into the water. Even more importantly, the physical act of writing breaks my train of thought, and I found that with this method of recording, I couldn't truly immerse myself in myself, if you get what I mean?

Now don't get me wrong, I think about 'stuff' all the time of course, about all sorts of subjects. I'm a thinker. Some might argue an over-thinker. That's just my nature. The problem I have with this, is that most situations during the working day, you're always distracted by other more mundane and less important interruptions. Like your job. And it's no better saving up your thinking time for when you're in bed at night. Another bad idea. You don't want your mind working on theories and formulations when you go to bed, you just want to sleep (though I keep a notepad and pen by my bed to jot things down if they occur, and if I think *they do warrant further consideration). So at this point I came up with the idea you know and seem to love; record my thoughts real-time. And at my most comfortable and natural. This was the genesis of 'The Man in the Bath.'*

From there, all it took was the correct bathroom angle for the camera on my phone, a little basic video editing software to pixelate my face and ensure there was no embarrassing nudity (more embarrassing for you than for me), add a title and there you have it. The video clips were created, and 'The Man in the Bath' was born into your World.

A Note: Just to correct and clarify what a few people have surmised on my messageboards, the pixilation was never originally for me to hide behind. Not in the way that has been suggested. I am proud of what and who I am. It was purely out of consideration for my family and workplace. I didn't know how this would go down back then, if anyone would notice, or if I would turn into a laughing stock. It could easily have happened that way if you hadn't all taken me to your hearts in the welcoming way that you did. And I was quite prepared for failure, but I didn't want to affect other people with my actions. That was the real reason why I hid my face. That, and the autograph hunters ;-)

As it turns out, and as we now know, this new identity of mine has now found its place in the wider world, and it seems that you like me. A lot of you do. So now, like Spiderman, and to ensure I am left in peace and unadulterated (to continue my messages to you), I continue to keep my real identity hidden. All I can say is that no-one has come close to guessing my corporeal equivalence so far, but do please feel free to speculate. It amuses me how wrong some of you are.

I know this little statement isn't particularly profound, which may disappoint a few of you, but it isn't supposed to be profound. It's what I say and not who I am that matters. I just thought that I should respond to the many questions you've been posting and save you asking the same questions over and over. This little missive is purely textual. Searchable on the site if you're interested in me, but not for general-interest consumption. You don't need to deconstruct me to benefit from my thoughts.

My next proper upload will be about the subject of spirituality and apples. Confused? Read on my children...
See you soon, on the messageboards and in the bath.

ManintheBath™ signing off.

Chp 2 – Dr David Dunn

"Fucking students!"

He muttered the words under his breath with venom, even though the door was shut and the office was empty. Sometimes saying it out loud helped, and there was a grim satisfaction in uttering the mantra. So David repeated it once more, for good measure.

"Fucking, fucking, students!"

Today wasn't so bad though. There were only fifty two messages in the e-mail inbox, and he <u>had</u> been out of the office for most of the morning, so it was only to be expected. But it was e-mails like this one that specifically irritated him:

Hi

I don't like the course I'm doing so I want to change to another one. the post coloneal lit one. thanks x

Licking his dry lips and popping a butternut squash flavoured sweet between his lips, David cracked his knuckles and clicked on 'reply.' This was supposed to be the cream of the country's academic high fliers.

Dear Moron,

It is usual to begin an official request by addressing your e-mail to a person, sometimes even by title, and to identify yourself at the end so that they know who it is making the request. Use my name, you fucking idiot! And the 'x' at the end? I'm sure that even <u>you</u> are not so fucking brainless as to think it appropriate to end an official missive with a 'kiss', so I presume this is your attempt at 'making your mark,' in the manner of the illiterate peasant from times past?

Use a capital letter at the beginning of a sentence. Spell the fucking words correctly. At least have the gumption to invent an excuse. You are making a formal request to one of the people with the power to screw up your degree for you. Though it would appear from your attempt at an e-mail that you are probably quite capable of doing that yourself. Now, please fuck off and attempt to grow a brain cell or two. And some manners as well, if it's not too much trouble?

When you manage that, write again politely in the correct format, using a spellcheck, and I'll think about it, you dumb shit-for-brains.

Yours Faithfully,
Dr David Dunn
Departmental Administrator, Liberal Arts Dept

With a slow exhalation of breath he leaned back in the chair to admire the neat and concise invective, before very carefully and deliberately deleting the message in its entirety, letter by letter. And then cancelling the remaining blank e-mail for good measure. It wouldn't do to send any of this accidentally. One day though... one day, he'd send it. On purpose.

David turned around in his chair to flick the switch on the kettle, before tackling the enquiry again, this time with all of his usual professional tact and diplomacy. It was amazing that seemingly intelligent teenagers... no, young adults... could be so thoughtless. The nagging memory of being one of them was crouching in the shadows at the back of his mind, laughing maniacally.

No, actually that wasn't quite true. He hadn't been one of 'these.' He *had* been a student once, true enough, but at least he'd had the decency and common sense to treat people in authority with some respect, outwardly at least. He'd been self-conscious at that point in life, having just moved from the outskirts of Penrith as a wide-eyed teenager, and had assumed that everyone in Leeds would be sophisticated and intelligent, and he'd worked for months on eradicating all signs of his own accent so that he could sound respectably 'RP.' He needn't have bothered, but that affectation had stuck. As a student, David had always been careful to show the proper respect for authority, feeling that it was a privilege to be in the company of his own intellectual superiors. Mind you, these days it seemed that any idiot who could spell their own name correctly could go to a University. Well, spell most of their name correctly, anyway. There was a very quiet knock on the door, followed by two more.

"Hello!"

David spoke loudly, waited a few seconds as usual, imagining the figure with an ear pressed to the door in the corridor, and then half-shouted the greeting a second time. The door swung slowly inwards, and a small grey head poked tentatively round, followed by a hand, which pushed a pair of tortoise-shell half-moon spectacles higher up the bridge of a nose. The long silver hair was then slicked back behind the left ear, where it stayed for a few seconds before flapping loose.

"Are you free? For a minute? It will only take a minute?"

David forced a practiced smile.

"Elias, yes of course. What can you do for me?"

A skinny, grey-suited body snaked around the door after the head and took a couple of paces before stopping, as though physically hit by a sudden apprehension.

"Oh yes... I see what you did there. Very good."

Professor Trelawn gave a tentative smile and held it, giving the appearance that he was waiting for approval. David couldn't help but smile back.

"Have a seat, please..."

"Thank you."

Rubbing his stomach with his right hand, the Professor shuffled forwards, his feet seeming to have difficulty in navigating the few required steps. His left hand came down to rest on the edge of the desk, leaving the scrawny body leaning at a very unusual angle. Professor Elias Trelawn was a long-standing member of the department, a nationally renowned expert in critical theory, and an extremely nervous man. He'd taught David as an undergraduate, had appeared ancient, even then. He seemed exactly the same today.

"The... err... could you tell me where I can find the student lists for the... errr... Derrida... errr..."

David's smile tightened and he interjected, to save a painful wait for the redundant end of the intended question.

"Of course. They were on the e-mail I sent you yesterday, Elias, and they're on the shared drive on the computer."

And on the e-mail that I sent you last week, and the one I sent to everyone the week before that. And on the paper copy which I put in your pigeonhole.

"Oh... really? I didn't see... erm..."

The surprise, as always, was perfectly genuine.

"Would you like me to print you out another copy?"

A smile of overwhelming relief spread out over the Professor's face.

"Would you? That would be exceedingly kind."

"Of course. Just give me a second."

David turned half-away to hide his expression and scowled as he located the document and hit the print key. It wasn't that Elias couldn't work computers as you might think. He was actually one of the more proficient lecturers when it came to matters of I.T. It just seemed to be a hobby of the academics here to be totally inept at anything vaguely organized or practical. David pondered, as he waited for the printer to finish, whether this was a sign of achievement in some secret academic coven; a sign that they had transcended the mundanities of everyday life. Perhaps they received some sort of badge or certificate when they reached the required level of physical ineptitude?

"Here you go."

He carefully placed the printed sheet directly into Elias' outstretched hand and waited. True to form, it took a moment or two before a startled expression appeared on the sprightly, lined face, which seemed to convey yet more surprise, that the hand he was looking at now magically held a piece of warm paper, with a list of the elusive student names.

"Thank you, thank you very much."

It was such a genuine and warm smile that any further thought of slapping him disappeared almost immediately. David cleared his throat as obviously and significantly as he could manage. To no reaction whatsoever, except for a quizzically raised eyebrow.

"So... Is there anything else I can do for you?"

"No, that was all, thank you very much Dr... er... David..."

Another slightly bewildered expression followed, before Elias slowly shook his head, and looked rather sheepish as it finally dawned that he was now supposed to be leaving the room.

"Thank you once again."

With the paper held up inches from the glasses, Professor Trelawn turned and shuffled towards the door, miscounting the steps, and banging his hand on the doorframe as he grasped for, and missed, the handle. He never looked up from the paper, but flailed his hand around for a second or two before finding the necessary knob and using it to open the door and leave. A soft "sorry" drifted through the closing door, as the exiting figure presumably walked into someone or something else.

David Dunn sighed as he stood up and reached for the jar of Nescafe. It was odd how nervous some of the members of staff were around him. Elias was nervous around everybody of course, but a number of the more established lecturers seemed to treat David's office like a holy shrine, acting overly polite and uncertain of what to say, or of how they should act. Granted, David *was* responsible for granting their expense claims, and had a significant input into the timetabling of their workloads, but some of these people had *taught* him, would remember the scruffy youth with the long hair and bad grammar who they'd graded and marked. Though he supposed that might perhaps have something to do with their nervousness. Maybe they were worried that he would remember, and exact revenge.

David snorted out loud. That had been a different him. If the eighteen year old Dave Dunn walked into this office now, he would probably either pity or scorn what he saw. And vice versa.

He grimaced. That wasn't a pleasant thought. Best not dwell on it.

The coffee (and coffee-mate powder) received a thorough stirring as David drifted off easily into the nebulosity of his own thoughts. The University had been run on vastly different lines back when he'd been an undergraduate. Tutorials held in the pub. Hand written grades. Grants. Fraternizing with students. Images and recollections flashed past, bringing a small smile.

There were many secrets and rumours from that time. He knew that the present regime would probably be very disapproving if they knew half of the knowledge to which he was privy, about the past history of some of the current staff. Drinking, smoking dope, affairs and sleeping with students aside (those things weren't *so* shocking or unusual for a University), injecting heroin in between lectures in the staff toilets, altering student's grades for sexual favours, pornographic home movies, writing student's assessed work for them. These things would cause quite a stir. And probably sackings in the current climate, though oddly, the staff members most directly connected to those stories seemed the least phased by David's re-appearance. And those distant shenanigans didn't bother David in the least either. It had made his student life so much more interesting. He almost pitied the current crop their bland and politically correct university experience.

David sat back down and scrolled through the fifty five messages now waiting, looking for the simple ones that would get the backlog down easily. It was only an hour to last until lunch. As he clicked absently through the inbox, removing the easiest-to-deal-with enquiries to a separate folder marked 'quickies,' he pondered the selection of sandwiches that would be available in the staff canteen, weighing the benefits of a healthy snack against the thought of a steak and ale pie from the pub. He promptly started wondering about the type of ale they used, how much was involved, and whether the pie was technically alcoholic.

Dave tried not to notice Nadine's legs. That proved to be exceedingly difficult. She was sitting on the barstool opposite, but just to the side of the table, and it seemed to him that Nadine had more legs than any woman had a right to. Not in number. She had the requisite number of legs, as the comedy sketch went, but they seemed to go upwards far further than you expected. She must surely have been aware, but was outwardly oblivious, to the effect of her calf-tautening black leather heeled boots, and very short but somehow oddly respectable skirts. They just made her legs seem even more incredibly lithe. Dr Nadine Silk was an extremely popular lecturer in the department.

The fact that her area of specialism was feminist literature somehow added to her appeal as a sexually desirable woman, rather than detracting from it. Among the students it was common knowledge that she was gay. Among the staff, it was common knowledge that she wasn't. And that arrangement seemed to satisfy Nadine just fine. She smiled slyly towards Dave in that coy, eye-lowering way she'd perfected, as she affected attention to the other male members of the Faculty seated around the large, oval table.

There wasn't a drinking culture any more, sadly, but the younger staff members, and some of the want-to-be-young lecturers, still met up every Friday night for drinks after work at a fairly quiet local pub, just off the main campus. One that was unpopular with the students. Dave couldn't help smiling back. He knew that the flirtation was nothing more than that, and equally knew that Nadine would receive a lighter workload than the other teachers the following semester. He also knew that none of them would complain. Nadine was quite remarkable in that she managed to naturally charm the opposite sex, but also remained on perplexingly good terms with the female members of staff. The fact that she would volunteer willingly to help out whenever needed made it seem churlish if anyone complained. And meant that rather than being overloaded with work she effectively got to choose exactly what she did and didn't do, in terms of administrative duties.

"What would anyone like? It's my round."

Nadine hadn't finished the question before three male lecturers, one married, one single, one with a girlfriend, all rose to their feet to argue that it was actually their turn to purchase the drinks. A quick, knowing glance from Nadine in Dave's direction brought disguised smirks to both their lips, hidden by a synchronised lifting of glasses. In a bizarre way, Dave felt proud that he knew Nadine would never sleep with him. It allowed him into a little circle of trust of two. They both knew exactly how their relationship worked, and rather than be threatened by his inside knowledge, she embraced it, and Dave received more attention as a result.

Nadine acquiesced to Tom's offer of a vodka and J2O, at the same time shifting slightly in her seat, and crossing her legs. The effect was a quite deliberate flash of forbidden inner thigh to Dave, hidden from their companions. She grinned and gave a broad smile of thanks to Tom, immediately turning her head back into a previous conversation, which left Tom standing alone for a moment, uncertain if he'd just received encouragement, or a brush off. That was one of the other things he liked about Nadine. Although they never discussed such matters, Dave prided himself on having a pretty good psycho-analytical mind. And Nadine was perverse as well as being beautiful and intelligent, all three being qualities which he very much admired. The deliberate flash of thigh flesh to Dave, hidden from the rest of the group by the table top, was her expression of contempt for the men on the other side of the table and their obvious try-hard desire for her. She'd only once alluded to this out loud, and then only obliquely, but it had stuck firm in his mind, one whispered comment when they'd been alone at the end of one of the Friday drinking sessions.

"I don't mind people finding me sexually attractive, Dave. I mean, for God's sake, who does? We're not supposed to say it as modern women, but we sometimes like being looked at too. I don't even particularly mind being leered at. Occasionally, when I'm in the mood, I sometimes even like it. But if a man hasn't got the nerve or inclination to actually ask me out, then why should I treat him any better than he treats me, or give him anything but the contempt he deserves? I'm sick of it. If they paid any attention to me above my chest, they might notice."

Then she'd giggled. Actually giggled. Not something anyone who worked with Dr Nadine Silk had ever heard before.

"I'm such a hypocrite! Oh well, who cares?"

He'd puzzled over that for quite some time, and though he couldn't fathom out the exact meaning, Dave finally settled on the fact that he'd been given an insight, and trusted above the other men. One day he'd actually ask her exactly what she'd meant, face to face. For now, the gift of trust was enough.

Nadine twisted slightly as she accepted the drink from Tyler Guthrie, who'd smoothly 'assisted' Tom in retrieving the drinks from the bar for just that purpose. Tyler was a well-built, chiselled, and distinctly married philosophy lecturer. Nadine nodded to him, her twisting motion quite deliberately flashing her thigh to Dave behind the tabletop once again, now becoming a code to show her contempt.

"...the effect is real enough... an action in one place can have consequences... bad or good... in another... don't you agree, Dave?"

He nodded with a deliberately bland expression as he turned to glance around the bar, so he could face away and grin openly. Life was good, despite the hassles of the work day. Things could be far worse.

#

David was more than a little drunk when he finally arrived back home, wandering along the river Aire for the view as he staggered, careful not to fall in. The evening had ended rather abruptly, after three youths (who had drunk far more than was comfortably required for an entertaining evening), had entered the pub and noisily taken centre-stage. Everyone had watched from the corners of their eyes, conversation subdued as a pervading sense of the inevitable seeped out over the occupants of the room. Soon enough, some innocuous remark had provoked offence, and this had prompted a bout of table pushing, raised voices, jostling, and threatened violence. It had all been over in a matter of minutes, with the offending drunks being strongly advised to leave, and shouting abuse at any drinker foolish enough to catch their eyes as they went, a glass being thrown petulantly to smash on the floor before the final exit. The incident had ruined the ambience of the evening, and as soon as the drinks on the table were finished, everyone had sloped off, somewhat deflated.

David flicked idly through the pages of his TV guide, but couldn't find anything that appealed, despite the numerous cable channels available. Sighing, he slid the wheeled computer table out from the corner of the lounge, and leaving a National Geographic documentary playing with the sound turned down, he fired up the desktop PC, pouring himself a small whisky and water while he waited for everything to load up. The computer was old and creaky, but still more rewarding than using his laptop, which didn't have the tactile reactions of a real keyboard.

Settling into the uncomfortable office-style chair, he imported a playlist of random songs into the media software, and started to flick idly through the favourites list of websites. He dismissed porn and sports in favour of a general community site that provided often humorous (and often pathetic) conversations on their messageboards. The intellectual content of the discussions was up (or rather 'down') to the usual standard, and to the strains of Limp Bizkit's cover of The Who's 'Behind Blue Eyes', David perused the latest threads. The main order of the day seemed to be the misdemeanours of political leaders, global warming (as usual), and maternity/paternity care arrangements (and why the government wasn't doing enough). One particular link did catch his eye though, a long, twenty-three page thread on the criminal justice system, focusing primarily on how rehabilitation was the order of the day. Cracking his knuckles, David hit 'new comment' and started to type.

Now, I'm not a Daily Mail reader, before you start. As a matter of fact I despise the hate-mongering little rag, but when will you people accept that jail is primarily a punishment? If you've ever had any experience of criminals you would know that most of the problems with crime come from serious offenders who have no intention of being rehabilitated. They know the system too well. It may surprise some of the bleeding-heart liberals on here to discover that the old adage 'crime doesn't pay' is actually a load of bollocks. It does pay. THAT'S WHY PEOPLE DO IT! It isn't rocket science to understand.

While the criminal justice system is so pre-occupied on human rights and rehabilitation (worthy subjects both), it is never going to be effective in the case of the persistent offenders who commit the majority of the serious crimes in our society.

David sipped at his whisky, and lit a cigarette while he gathered his argument, nodding his head along to the rhythmic thump of a Nine Inch Nails track, and then typing in time with it.

Young criminals learn early that if you or your lawyer know the system, then you can offend pretty much at will for a hell of a long time before a custodial sentence is even a serious possibility. In the meantime, the first-time offender, who genuinely could in all actuality be discouraged or rehabilitated, will in all probability suffer the consequences of not playing the system, and will receive an unduly harsh sentence. At the same hearing, the habitual criminal may be sent to a young offender's institution where they lose their right to freedom, granted. But they also receive frequently better accommodation and care than they would at home, spend all their time with like-minded people, swapping tips and stories and encouraging each other in a finishing school for young scrotes. Hardly a deterrent.

They may receive training and 'opportunities' to help them change their ways. How exactly does that help now? Wouldn't it be better to provide the training or opportunities in their life on the outside beforehand, to avoid the offending in the first place, if that's the intended solution? When they get out, do you honestly believe they'll find a job just because their incarceration is spelled correctly on their freshly designed CVs?

Here's a novel idea. Make jails and offenders' institutions a punishment! The lack of televisions, computers, good food, comfort, a gym, and day trips for criminals, do not constitute an abuse of human rights in my book! Make them not want to come back instead. These people are quite used to police cells so give them a small, sparse room, plain bed, and plain, healthy food. If they want entertainment then teach them to read and give them books. If they want to earn privileges like television or organised sport, then let them _earn_ it through work, training, or education. And believe it or *not, you don't need access to computer games, or the internet, to learn!*

Punishment means punishment, people! If you want to keep more individuals out of jail then provide them with opportunities before they get there, or when they get out, if they really want them, and ask <u>voluntarily</u>! You can lead a horse to water etc... Jail is jail. Bad people go there. To be punished and to keep them off the streets. Here endeth the lesson.

Nodding with satisfaction that he had made his point, David hit 'post' and drained the glass, moving to the mantelpiece and opening the small wooden box that contained his pot, so he could roll a joint before bed. The wildlife documentary on the TV had finished so he turned the speakers on the computer off, and flicked the remote onto Radio Four for some background education, while he started to build.

#

David woke up on the sofa with a very dry mouth. The radio was still playing, and the carriage clock on the mantle said 3am. Licking his parched lips, he forced himself to his feet and staggered uncertainly towards the kitchen to turn on the kettle.

As it started to boil, David finally noticed the flickering glow coming from the still-active PC screen in the corner of the room. As he reached for the mouse to turn off the computer, he saw the substantial number of additional posts made to the thread which he'd never bothered to navigate away from. Blinking and yawning, he sat down and started to absently browse through, to see if anyone had bothered to reply directly to his points.

The kettle boiled and switched off in the background, but David didn't notice as he became engrossed in the virtual conversation he'd just slept through. There were a couple of predictable posts accusing him of being heartless, and one that provoked a chuckle by comparing him to Hitler (Godwin's Law), but the original post seemed to have sparked off a genuine two page follow-on of replies discussing his ideas, with a variety of contributors responding and debating. One comment in particular, from the site moderator, made David smile in self-satisfaction.

I presume you've logged off for the evening but thank you. It's nice to hear a straightforward and forthright opinion that provokes debate. I might not agree with

#

The next morning he felt a slight twinge of embarrassment about the online rant. Not about having *done* it; to be honest there was a wonderful sense of achievement that he'd gotten something off his chest, and that a number of people had listened, and taken the time to respond. No, it was more that, thinking about what he'd actually written, those ideas weren't really David's true opinions, they were the whisky's. At least he hoped they weren't his. True, he did have strong feelings on crime and punishment, but those weren't quite as cut and dried as he'd made out last night. He'd been arrested once himself, for little more than stupid drunken, youthful, student exuberance, and he wouldn't like to think that he was living in a world where something as insignificant as that could result in a criminal record. Or a small, square room and no TV.

These were the thoughts wandering around the brain of David as he got dressed and ready for work. It wasn't technically a work day, but he lived quite close to the campus, and it was a labour and sanity-saving routine which had developed over the last few years. The simple act of going into the office and clearing through the lower level papers on the desk, and messages in the inbox (the ones he couldn't face last thing on a Friday and definitely didn't want to face first thing on a Monday morning), and the fact he could get rid of them in an uninterrupted hour or two made the beginning of the following week more bearable. As they were lower level chores, while his body worked, his mind was still on the weekend, free to do what it liked. It was an oblique justification but it worked for David. And today, right now, his mind decided that the appropriate thing to do was wander. And then to wonder if any of the stray thoughts he fixated on might be suitable to upload onto the discussion messageboards later.

David was a thinker. Not necessarily a deep thinker all the time, but he was cursed with the ability, or the necessity, to consider certain ideas at length. A stray thought would lodge in his head and he wouldn't be able to shake it until he'd explored it exhaustively from every angle. It was a bit like getting a song lyric stuck in your brain and not being able to forget it, however appealing the idea might be or however hard you might try. It had always been the same for him, since he was a small child. That was also the reason that, unlike many of his acquaintances, David enjoyed his own company. It gave him the uninterrupted freedom to indulge his mind.

One of David's previous girlfriends had once told him that she didn't like spending time on her own, found it boring, and that admission had provoked a good few hours' thought in itself. How could you not like your own company? Surely if you didn't like yourself then you couldn't expect anyone else to, either? That was the conclusion he'd finally come to. After that conclusion, he'd started to notice the unlikeable things about the girl himself. And had promptly dumped her. The last he'd heard, Carla was married with two children and living in Harrogate. David was still single.

Today, it was mostly low level and insignificant things that decided to occupy his mind. While he had been actively trying to think about big topics he could contribute his considered opinions on, his mind decided instead, that the topic of fingernails would catch his attention. It was a subject which had always intrigued him a little, but never enough to actively find the answer; where do fingernails actually start? Or rather, how do they start?

As he filed away the correspondence and finance documents, David kept looking closely at his hands and pressing one finger to the back of the other. Did they start in a straight solid line under the skin or was there a malleable fleshy transition from finger to fingernail? He knew they could be pulled out, and that suggested there must be a specific end to a fingernail, but how far back did it go? How did it end? It was then that his eyes were drawn to the pale semi-circle at the back of his thumbnails. And he kept looking at them. It had never occurred before, but if you actually look at fingernail semi-circles for more than a second or two, they actually appear very strange.

David was distantly aware that the semi-circles were something to do with calcium and minerals, but of more pressing concern was the fact that he couldn't see circles on the nail of every finger. This disturbing revelation provoked a pause, and a pushing back of the skin on top of each fingernail until he could find the shape beneath. He continued until he was sure that, however small, there was a semi-circle showing on every nail. David sighed. This was one of those things. It was going to be a recurrent obsession all through the day, he could tell. It would be with him until he finally fell asleep, exhausted from his exploration.

Chp 4 – Sunday

It was such a relief to wake up and be able to turn the alarm off without guilt, and just lie there. It was a beautiful moment. Best part of the day; not have to worry or think about work at all. So quite naturally, David Dunn spent the next fifteen minutes having his brain overtaken with unexpected thoughts about his job; which documents hadn't yet been completed? How a particular personnel problem could be best approached? What still needed to be done prior to the examinations period?

At eight-sixteen a.m. David gave up trying to go back to sleep and kicked off the duvet, grumpily stomping through to the kitchen area to make a coffee, before heading for the daily ritual of brushing, washing, and emptying. He listed the day's main duties in his head as he went through the motions, and the order in which they would be performed. Even plans such as 'surf the net' were given an approximate timescale, and the important questions of which beer to buy, and which biscuits might be needed to dunk in tea that evening for supper; all were given due time and consideration.

After the food shopping (plus lightbulbs and binliners) had been physically completed and put away in cupboards, he loaded the washing machine with work clothes, some socks and underwear, and sat down to watch late-morning television with a cup of milky coffee. It was at that point some unknown force prompted David's mind to remember about, and then fixate on, the files on his old computer backup drives. The memory of them flicked into his mind from nowhere, as memories sometimes did. But once a thought like that appeared it could rarely be shaken until he'd done something about it.

Ten minutes later, David was sitting on the floor, searching through a box of detritus that had never been unpacked since moving in five years earlier, doggedly looking for the backup drive he thought he remembered. The house off Roundhay Park had been bigger, but less convenient for work, and since the downsizing there were still a number of stored and never re-opened cardboard boxes in the closet behind the rarely-used hoover. A further fifteen minutes, another box and two shelves later, and he was laying on the settee with the laptop on his thighs, looking through the files.

David had no clue where the concept had originally come from, but on one particular evening six years previously, he had become obsessed with the notion that that many of his most interesting flights of fancy, thoughts and ideas, occurred in one of two places; either while driving a familiar route which he only needed one part of his brain to concentrate on, or in the bath. As he no longer had a car, his attention had been ostensibly on the bath.

This fixation had gestated over a number of days, had developed into a plan, and he'd made several abortive attempts to write up his observations and revelations as soon as he got out of the tub. At first, he'd tried carrying a notebook and pen to accompany his soak in real-time, then tried utilising a Dictaphone, to better record his thoughts as they actually occurred. It was a methodical process of elimination, to discover the most effective method of retaining and recording his own genius. These attempts had all proved to be unsatisfying solutions for practical reasons, and though the next methodology seemed in hindsight to be an almost natural progression, he couldn't for the life of him recall what had prompted the fairly unorthodox solution to his quandary. David had decided to try and video himself, while actually in the process of taking his bath. He owned a state-of-the-art phone that also acted as both a video camera and webcam (complete with tripod), and after a little experimentation, had found a location on the windowsill where he could film himself from the waist up to retain his modesty, without condensation steaming up the lens.

The next time David had taken his nightly bath, he'd switched on the video camera function first, already in the mood to philosophise. He lay on the couch and surfed through the various backup discs now, his obsessive tendencies meaning he didn't just want, but needed, to find those videos. His own memories brought back images of awkwardly covering his private parts from the camera as he got in and out of the water, and of having to 'force' thoughts into vocalisations for the first couple of times he'd tried this experiment. But David had been determined. And on the third evening, exhausted from work, he'd closed his eyes once he was neck deep in the hot, soapy water, almost oblivious to his intended task. That was when he remembered feeling his mind start to wander in a more usual and natural way, and he'd started to talk out loud, creating what he was sure now had been quite an interesting little monologue to camera.

As soon as David had finished that first recording, he'd transferred the short video clip to his computer, and watched it back himself about an hour later. He recalled being slightly embarrassed at his flabby, naked form at the beginning and end of the footage, but knew that he'd also found himself smiling as he'd watched his video clip continue, impressed with some of the content and humorous delivery. He'd been very satisfied with his initial creation.

Subsequently, David had filmed himself regularly for perhaps a month during his nightly soaks. Playing them back, he'd discovered more and more pearls of his own wisdom, or so he thought, in amongst the often rambling and frequently incoherent other addresses to the camera. He'd started to edit and organise the video files thematically, cutting out the parts of his climbing in and out of the tub, and the occasionally nonsensical introductions.

That was when he'd picked the very best videos out, and had tried an experiment to make a more coherent and viewable experience. He'd used his computer to add title graphics to a short two minute edited segment, calling it 'Man in the Bath,' in a moment of inspired practicality. And then...

And then, David hadn't known what to do with the end product. Putting that problem aside for later, he'd made yet more edited and titled clips, as the creation was enjoyable in itself, and it gave him a warm glow to watch his own thoughts back onscreen, and agree with them. And he'd started to play around with his new video blurring software, to make himself truly anonymous, just a voice or truth.

Shortly afterwards, he'd met Cathy. The lovely Cathy. And like so many other ideas David Dunn had started, he'd shelved the video project for a rainy day; stored, filed and saved to backup computer discs.

Now, plumping up a cushion behind him with a smile, he found the folder he'd been searching for, sighed with the satisfaction of completing the hunt, sipped at his hot milky coffee, and pressed play on the first of his old video files, hoping they'd be as good as he remembered them to be.

Chp 5 – Man in the Bath
(recording the first 'successful' video clip)

The camera was running, and David closed his eyes and sank under the bubbles for a few seconds, coming up for air with a loud gasp, and slicking his shoulder-length brown hair back, to plaster it against his skull, in the process revealing a severely receding Dracula hairline. He blinked a couple of times and settled his arms over the edges of the bath.

"So... 'Man in the Bath' here... Hi... today's lecture is... no, hang on, start again..."

David licked his lips, tasting the unpleasant tang of Radox, and scraped his tongue back along his upper teeth to try and remove the lingering sensation. He smacked his lips theatrically and turned his head directly towards the phone/video camera, resting on its small tripod on the top of the washing basket (this proved to be a better angle than the window sill). He cleared his throat and tried vocalising a few phrases out loud, to check that his voice and accent wouldn't be recognisable. He nodded contentedly to himself at the bland RP coming back.

"So... 'Man in the Bath' here... Hi... today's thought is... the Beatles... the fifth Beatle... who was it?"

David paused, for a suitably dramatic and intentional effect.

"So... who was the apocryphal fifth member of The Beatles? I took a straw poll at work today and the most popular name that sprung to the minds of the people I asked was Pete Best, the original drummer. The other two receiving votes were Stuart Sutcliffe, and Mike McGear - McCartney's brother. Not sure why that was. So I thought it was worth considering the different applicants for the post; and, in no particular order... one, Mike McGear – no. That's simply a no. His latter association with McGough and the Phantom Flan Flinger, in The Scaffold, means that he should be automatically stricken from any and all music history immediately, if not sooner. Besides which, I have no idea why he got the vote anyway, as he was never in The Beatles. Option two, Pete Best – certainly has a claim as a founder member, of sorts, though his claim seems to rest mainly on the fact his mum had money and a van, without which they probably wouldn't have got to the venues. Three, Stuart Sutcliffe – a good claim, genuine member of the band, bassist, talented and creative, in terms of art anyway, toured with them pre-fame.

Also Lennon's best mate. Four, Brian Epstein – certainly contributed to their early success, but I don't think his contribution was unique enough to rate a fifth Beatlehood. Five, George Martin – his 'sound' certainly helped The Beatles reach their creative peak, and arguably the strongest musical claimant to the throne. Six, Astrid whatserface - Kircher or something? Sutcliffe's girlfriend. In her re-styling of the band from leather-jacketed, pornclad, house band whizzkids, to the moptop suited group who found acceptance and the opportunity to flourish, her influence can't be over-rated. Seven, Klaus whathisname – keyboardist, designer... the Revolver cover I think, though I could be wrong."

A frown rippled over David's brow.

"...vague feeling he may have shagged Astrid after Sutcliffe popped his clogs... maybe they got married, that would explain the similarities with the surname of 'whatshername'... anyway, a key member at times, helping them develop and stay together, but a bit of a no-mark, if you'll excuse the scouse terminology, when it comes to being 'An actual Beatle.' So no. Eight, Alan White – drummer on the U.S. tour, and part of the band for a while. But then again so were others like Billy Preston on the odd occasion, so White's contribution isn't unique enough for him to score highly on my Beatle-ometer. Nine, Yoko – we're not necessarily just talking musical contribution, so the influence of Yoko Ono could give her a claim, though admittedly mainly being the conduit of dissatisfaction and an already existing fractiousness. No."

Settling easily into his narrative flow now, David brushed at the foam that had somehow found its way onto his nose, and paused to gather his train of thought into a more coherent structure and direction.

"No, all the above have a claim of some kind, but my own candidate for the title of fifth Beatle, and this might be controversial... hear me out... my 'fifth Beatle' would be a young man by the name of Mark Chapman! Now, before rabid Lennonites attempt to 'do a Chapman' on *me*, remember that the Beatles were very highly regarded during the Seventies but weren't the incredible all-worshipful force they are today. It was Chapman's assassination of Lennon that propelled them back to the limelight, and a dead martyr always helps to give fame. Ask Jesus. Though not about The Beatles. I think they pissed Him off enough. But I'm getting off track. Where was I...? Oh yes, dissing The Beatles and Lennon... particularly Lennon, yes, he's over-rated. If you don't believe me, look at the turgid piece of drivel that is

'Imagine.' It limped awkwardly to number 6 in the mid-seventies, powered by a loyal fanbase, and was then promptly forgotten by most. No, don't try and re-write history, think back to the actual time, or look it up if you're not old enough. 'Imagine' was largely pushed into the bargain-bin of also rans until Chapman shot Lennon, when it's weedy schoolboy poetry lyrics created a new generation who thought Lennon was the Messiah. Helped at the this point by the fact he was dead, which is always an assistance to a Messiah."

David couldn't help smiling to himself at this point. Then frowning slightly at the fact he'd just repeated himself with another Jesus reference, lessening the intended joke.

"... don't get me wrong... I don't dislike Lennon per se, and I love some of his music, but if he hadn't died, he would be much less highly regarded. Be honest, he didn't half produce some crap in the seventies! ...*and* laboured under the misapprehension that his Aunt Mimi had raised him as a working class boy. No, John, no! The words you are looking for are overbearing middle-class wife-beating loudmouth."

David's fingers lifted over his chest and steepled into an upside down 'V' of contemplation, as the 'Man in the Bath' was momentarily distracted by the sight of his own tattoo, something he was constantly surprised by, even to this day, twenty odd years after it had been inked onto him. He forced his eyes away before his mind could decide on a trip down that particular memory lane. That could wait for another night, and another bath.

"... now, The Beatles were pretty unusual. There aren't many bands that can have four members write hit songs; the only other one I can think of offhand is Queen. And three of the songwriters in The Beatles were excellent. I think a lot of people who appreciate the music without bias will agree, that they wrote in quite different but equally admirable ways. George Harrison was, I think, probably the best and most innovative of the three. Lennon knew what worked and could hook into popular feeling better than most other songwriters. And McCartney was, and is, a musical chameleon, probably the most versatile of the lot. I hated Wings, but his post-Beatles work was astounding really. It encompassed Mull of Bloody Kintyre - annoying, kitsch, hugely successful and a musical change in direction-, the Frog song thing, banned protest songs about the Irish - far more radical and daring at the time than anything Lennon did-, and classical and white label dance music. He showed a real lack of fear of new directions or experimentation and was surprisingly good in some of those I just said."

He tried not to let the frown show, knowing that the end of the previous sentence had been less than eloquently put.

"This may surprise you, but I'm not going to knock Ringo here. I'd compare him to John Deacon of Queen. Both were lower profile, both actually did write successful and popular songs – yes, they did, go and look if you don't believe me- but both, far more importantly, were integral to the sound and spirit of their bands. Without them, the dynamic would have been very different and who knows what would have resulted?"

David noticed the blinking icon showing that the battery was starting to fade, and decided to speed up the conclusion of this particular monologue. He looked directly back into the small camera lens.

"... but to go back to my original point, the 'historic' fifth Beatle should probably be Sutcliffe, the 'musical' fifth Beatle is undoubtedly George Martin, the 'artistic' fifth Beatle is arguably Astrid whatsername. But in terms of being the biggest influence overall, it has to be Mark Chapman. Even if you don't believe my reasoning about the resurgence, re-evaluation, and martyrdom of Lennon, Chapman did undoubtedly put a stop to their ever being a re-union. And thus sealed their place as a historically truly 'great' band, rather than a very good band who are still around and could reform, and disappoint people who try to convince themselves deludedly that it's going to be the same as the band's heyday - Velvet Underground, Sex Pistols, Led Zep, The Doors, please stand up and take a bow, or hide your faces in shame, except Zep ..."

David made a deliberately contemplative face, though it wouldn't be seen in the finished film. By now he already had the idea that he would anonymise the finished product.

"...they were still good actually – but back to the matter and murderer in hand...Chapman... he was misguided certainly, but I still think that in terms of influence, Mark Chapman is undoubtedly the closest thing there is to a 'fifth Beatle.' Added to which, he popularised 'Catcher in the Rye' to a new generation, and it's rather a good book!"

Another smile at the camera. Not necessary of course, as his entire head would be blurred out to avoid recognition, but it felt good, and *he* would know he'd smiled.

"Here endeth the lesson. 'Man in the Bath,' signing off... until next time..."

Chp 6 – Work and Upload

The e-mails, phone calls, and knocks on the door were even more annoying than usual today. In bed last night, fresh from watching the impressive old clips, David had started to develop a plan, deciding that he should do something to fulfil his clear potential as a video philosopher. He'd mentally worked through all the options and technicalities carefully, and had formulated a timescale and plan, as was his wont. Today he was trying to plan how to knock off the rough edges to his scheme, and perfect this wonderful new project.

He slid to his feet and grabbed the 'do not disturb' sign, hanging it over the handle on the outside of the door, then pulled out a file of finance forms which needed indexing, a job he'd put off for several months, but which was mechanical and mindless enough to suit his current intentions.

The 'Man in the Bath' clips were actually very good, he'd decided. They were funny (he thought so, anyway), they were a bit different, and there was always a market on the internet for the novelty these days. *And* there were some genuinely interesting ideas and insights there, worthy of a far wider audience. There were insights and clever word-plays that he hadn't even noticed at the time of actual recording, which had just slipped into his narratives 'mid-flow,' but which had really impressed the present-day David on re-watching. Other audiences would no doubt appreciate them too. Amongst the bath-based rants he'd rediscovered (some, it seemed, *were* virtual rants on the subjects of whatever had been bugging him on that particular day), were longer espousals of philosophy, religion, and several speeches relating to the big themes of life and death, and 'the meaning of it all.' Very interesting stuff. Yes, he mused, you could always find a good audience for material like that.

There had also been several quite vitriolic episodes containing his views on women. He'd been a little shocked and had to remind himself that these hadn't been his genuine views, they'd been cathartic rants after arguments or frustrations with specific female friends or lovers. With that remembered, those clips had been particularly liberating to watch again, as David remembered full well the individual situation that had given rise to every speech. While they might undoubtedly seem quite vicious and misanthropic to the casual viewer who didn't know the context, they had all been related to specific events involving individual women, and he remembered feeling much better having vocalised and released his complaints or frustrations out loud.

These verbal barrages had rarely been prompted by mundanities such as rejection or conflict with David himself though, in fact, quite the opposite. Each thinly-veiled attack rant (and let's be honest, that's what they essentially were) had followed a conversation with a female, usually where David had been the sympathetic shoulder to cry on, or ear to sob into, where he'd said 'the right thing' he knew the other party had wanted to hear, or advice he didn't mean or believe, designed purely to comfort. His videos on these subjects had been what he'd *actually* wanted to say at the time but hadn't dared.

The reason he hadn't dared is that David's real genuine and unuttered feelings invariably contained at least some sense that the woman in question had been in the wrong herself, had been misguided, or simply foolish, but you couldn't say that to a woman's face when she was upset, however kindly-meant. Instead, the unuttered views each became the germ for a 'Man in the Bath' espousal, on the foolishness or hypocritical nature of women in general. Some of the videos had been about very personal events which the individual women had experienced and shared with him, though the content of his monologues was never enough to reveal their actual identities. The 'sermons' he gave usually related what a woman in that situation *should* have done or said, if she'd had any sense, composure, or the objectivity that he himself had. In truth, he genuinely *did* want the women he knew to have done or said the things he suggested in his rants. To have been strong. To have taken control. The videos had been through frustration.

He had found himself laughing out loud in lots of places when he'd watched those particular clips back last night though. Partly with amusement at his own, clearly genuine, indignation, and partly at his own cleverness, as he'd recognised at least a kernel of truth and genuine insight into what he thought of as the female psyche. He'd felt vindicated about a couple of the specific rants, where he was fairly certain that he remembered the women in question subsequently confiding to him that they wished they'd acted things differently themselves. David thought of himself as satisfied by that, rather than smug.

There had been a video he'd made on the subject of 'mansplaining' too, where he'd slowly and deliberately condescended (with a tongue firmly in the cheek) that women shouldn't confuse compound words with the wisdom he brought from a man's insightful perspective. He'd laughed, watching that video back, but had reluctantly deleted the file, knowing he should never risk letting another person see that. In the current climate, if someone took that seriously, he could be in real physical danger from half the population.

Those hadn't been the Man in the Bath clips which had inspired his current plans though, not those personal ones. It had been the broader, more wide-reaching philosophies and thoughts on the current state of the world which he'd decided he wanted to share. Watching them back, there were nuggets of universal wisdom, observations of unnoticed hypocrisies, thoughts which might benefit everybody.

Yes, the existing 'philosophy' clips definitely had something going for them, even if they still suffered from too much rambling and digression in places. That could be improved with some judicious editing. He had a lot of footage in total, plenty to pick from, and it would be a shame to waste the best of his monologues. Plus, he could always make more, if needed. Practice makes perfect.

David's mind meandered gradually back to his current location as he realised that his concentration had drifted once again, away from the true task at hand. There were practical issues for him to consider. What were the next steps, and how would he achieve the ultimate goal of effectively disseminating his video wisdom? That was what he should be focussing on, while his hands continued to complete the menial paperwork on auto-pilot.

A loud rap echoed from the door, followed by three more, snapped him out of his contemplations. David reached for the phone receiver. His memory ticked through the recognisable calling routine of the different staff, and quickly came to the hallmark four knocks of Dr Simon Temple, affectionately known as 'Saint.' David held his breath, and the phone to his ear as a justification for delaying the encounter, if the visitor continued to ignore the 'Do Not Disturb' sign on the door.

A further knock came again a few seconds later, and David judged it prudent to escalate his deception, inventing and loudly delivering, one end of a conversation which was clearly supposed to be with a student, on a confidential matter. He pictured the Saint with his ear pressed up against the wood, listening and hearing his words, knowing this would be the exact scene on the other side of the door. Receding footsteps followed, and David exhaled in relief, replacing the unused phone receiver. The Saint would want to discuss the agenda for the next departmental strategy meeting, and it would be a protracted, involved, and annoying discussion, which could easily wait until the following day. David pulled out some finance coding slips and started to fill in the first, completing overdue invoice payments.

Number one issue to deal with, was of course, anonymity. David was quite prepared to let people see the videos, and the fact he was in the bath while speaking didn't concern him in the least, from a personal point of view. He knew that he had a position of some small respectability and responsibility though. And more specifically, someone he knew, one of the students for example, might see them, which, as he was appearing naked, might undermine his authority in the University. So, the first order of the day would be to anonymise all of the clips more effectively. There was a free pixelation program he'd received on the cover-disc of a computer magazine, and this would be far more effective and efficient than the crude and patchy blurring he'd managed on his existing attempts. There had been a tutorial in the magazine, and all it would apparently need was a short macro to identify and cover his face consistently. That should be sufficient. David was quite I.T. literate for an Arts person.

The clips were short, and the video editing software he had mastered for another project would easily edit and convert clips small enough to upload, and keep the attention of the casual viewer for a few minutes. With a little experimentation, more judicious pruning of the less coherent ramblings, and a nice colour title fading in and out, the end result would be smoother and more professional than his first attempts back at the old house, in the old bath. Yes, that could be quite effective.

David found himself grinning as he lifted the next piece of paper. It was a complicated payment that had been returned from the finance office already, because one section had a crossing-out that hadn't been initialled. The smile turned to a scowl, and he initialled the paper with an angry pen flourish, pushing it roughly back into an internal envelope, and marking the return address in capitals with the red biro he favoured for jobs like this. The next invoice was another complicated one, which had been raised by a rival administrator in another University department. This one got stuffed to the bottom of the pile, mentally noted with a 'when I get chance and am in a good mood' post-it.

A softer knock at the door took David's attention, and this sound he instantly recognised as belonging to Nadine.

"Hi!"

It was a bright, welcoming tone of voice that he found himself using in answer to the knock. The door opened and David strained to keep his eyeline above the hips and short skirt as the slim figure entered. Today, she was wearing quite a formal grey jacket and sweater top underneath. This had quite the unintended effect of making the colour rise in David's cheeks, and forcing his eyes to lift higher, above the chest, as quickly as possible. The librarian look, and snugness of the sweater definitely suited Nadine. He greeted the eyes he met with a warm and welcoming smile.

"What can I do to you?... I mean *for* you...?"

He swiftly added a wink to cover the unintentional and quite Freudian slip, hoping that she'd think it was just part of the usual flirtatious banter. Nadine sat down without invitation. A sudden image of her in the bath flashed into David's mind ,and he had to physically shake his head to dislodge the image as fast as possible.

"'You okay?"

A queer little smile spread across her subtly lipsticked lips as she asked, and Dave nodded quickly.

"'Course. Sorry. My mind was miles away. What can I do for you today?"

She started to talk, and David paid half his attention to her as his mind returned to thoughts of her in his bath. It was partly to stop his eyeline slipping lower, along with thoughts of suds, that David forced the half of his mind not listening to her words to think about something else. About the remaining practicalities of pixelating a moving face. He partially succeeded, gripping onto complex image-manipulation issues as tightly as possible, to stop himself picturing the actual bath and a naked Nadine.

"I can go away and come back later if you want?"

That brought his attention back sharply. Although the tone of voice favoured wry humour, there was a hint of threat that he detected, or imagined, along the lines of: *'I'm not wasting good flirtation if I don't have your full attention and if you're not going to react.'*

David's train of thought had unintentionally lodged firmly onto the thorny issues of intelligent pixilation quite deeply though. He was almost tempted to agree. Until his eyes caught the shape of the sweater again, and David wrested his total attention back to the woman on the other side of the desk.

There were several other interruptions and with each one, the sharpness in his responses and the well cultivated, 'I'm busy, be quick' tone, grew more dominant. But in the moments between the visitors and phone calls, the plan was now taking definite shape. E-mails had been quickly discarded as an ineffective vehicle for the clips, and David had settled on some form of website as the best delivery method for the sermons of the Man in the Bath. Sermons. That was the most satisfying terminology he'd considered so far. Preaching to the unconverted and unenlightened.

A staff meeting at 2pm had provided the perfect cover for further mental investigation of the project. Ostensibly there as a minute taker, David usually became a significant contributor to these meetings. In this particular case, the meeting considered the strategy for attracting a wider ethnographic spread to future intakes of students, or alternatives to explain why such a policy wouldn't work (which he already knew it wouldn't but couldn't be bothered to explain today). A Dictaphone on the table provided the perfect insurance against non-attention, and David was already up to speed on all the arguments, so as long as he made a few token comments, and kept a general track of the conversation, he could let his mind do its thing elsewhere. A management-speak quotation of University policy would always distract and confuse the academics present if David was roused, and most of them would take his word as gospel, at least for long enough for him to rediscover what was being talked about.

While that meeting was going on, David could complete his own mental agenda, starting with a fundamental point, was it worth continuing with this idea at all? He examined a pre-prepared pro's and con's list, ignoring the babble of background sounds discussing the less important issues about the students. The question in hand was whether anyone would actually pay any attention to, or even see, the video clips. This doubt was easily countered, as the whole project hadn't ever been intended as an ego-trip. It was more of an experiment. It genuinely didn't matter to him whether anyone else actually saw the films or not, so long as he'd put all the pieces in place for it to be a success, and had completed his plan. If the project was followed through to its natural conclusion, and that he could judge it as a completed process and move on, which was satisfying in itself. Question one answered; he would continue and finish what he'd started. David always started to begin a list with something he could mark off quickly as achieved, and he'd known the answer to this question before he'd asked himself. But the asking was part of the methodology, part of the process.

Mental bullet point two; method of delivery and platform? Answer: a free website. Little administration needed, minimum effort, maximum effect. A simple template webpage would suffice, possibly a text blog if he was feeling extravagant, and anyone started visiting the site for real.

David was snapped out of his reverie for a moment, just as that nice, neat, solution occurred. It seemed that he'd been asked a specific question, and the figures around the table were waiting for an answer. He threw back a suitably vague 'one-fit' statement, to claim a moment of thought in which he could work out what the specific question had been.

"Does that fit with the official policy of the University? And didn't someone suggest something remarkably similar last year?"

The first query was a useful catchall statement that was guaranteed to prod at least one orator to life, always did. The second question was true for 95% of suggestions made in meetings like this one, as almost every proposal had been considered at some point in the past. It would stir up old arguments for a while until he was ready to turn his full attention back to the room. The two comebacks did their trick, as expected. David shared a sly look with Nadine (who seemed unnaturally aware of the little devices he regularly employed), as one of the more vociferous professors took the opportunity to expound his own views, and drag the conversation further away from the original topic of discussion, just as David had hoped.

Mental bullet three. Or 2b, to be accurate; details of the website. David controlled the departmental web space himself, and it would be a quite straightforward process to open a small new set of pages from one of the little used research web-accounts, that only he monitored. He'd once briefly dated a girl who worked in the I.T. department, and had accidentally learned a little trick from her, so he knew the backdoor method of using webspace without it showing up on any official records or audits. The 'Man in the Bath' could be born. Job done. Halfway down the only agenda that mattered. But first...

David butted back into the academics' conversation triumphantly, with a broad smile, dragging the details of the half-heard debate back into his conscious mind, and suddenly remembering the individual who had made the same suggestion to this very meeting, twelve months ago. Dr Williams scowled. Apologising insincerely for his interruption, David fought to remove the smile from his lips as he innocently asked the scowling face in his most deadpan voice, whether Dr Williams had ever followed up on the action point from the equivalent meeting held the previous year. Wasn't there a written outline proposal that Dr Williams had agreed to send around for further discussion at that point, to propose specific details to the committee? David apologised again, for the fact it was easy to forget these things with so much going on, but he could add the action point again if it would be helpful, for further discussion at the next meeting? No-one but Nadine seemed to notice it wasn't an apology at all.

"Hi, Man in the Bath here. Let's jump straight to the point today, shall we? Porn... good thing, or a bad thing?"

The figure smoothed back his wet hair and settled into a more comfortable position, with his arms resting on the edges of the bath. He templed his fingers in a thoughtful pose, knowing this would be mostly blocked by the pixilation, but also knowing that it would help him relax into a suitable frame of mind to espouse.

"...let's bypass the more general arguments about pornography. I'm quite sure you have your own strong opinion on those, and that it is unlikely to be altered by anything a mere naked figure-torso like me might put forward, but what I was specifically wondering was... is porn a feminist issue? Or perhaps more accurately, should porn be seen as a pro-feminist issue?"

A pause to let that sink in.

"Now, I don't know if you're aware, but over recent years there has been a sea-change in pornography. And I don't just mean in terms of availability, I mean in terms of subject, tone, and delivery... and let me be straight about this, before I start. I'm sitting comfortably in the pro-pornography camp. I love porn. There, I've said it. I think porn is great."

The Man in the Bath held a 'thumbs up' pose with both hands for a moment, to visually emphasize his approval.

"But there is a big split in modern pornography..."

He almost blushed.

"...if you'll excuse the phrase... what I meant is that there is a divide... on one side is the traditional 'plastic tits,' bad dialogue, gynaecological camp of movies; 'traditional porn', if you will. Not good in my book, by the way. In the opposing camp, there is the relatively new phenomenon of widespread, so-called 'gonzo' porn. A little sidebar here for the uninitiated. 'Gonzo' does not refer to the muppet with the long nose, though that does suggest quite interesting new possibilities for pornography... no, 'gonzo,' at its most basic, means 'home made' or 'realistic.'"

The Man in the Bath paused for another appropriate 'gather your thoughts' moment, and to allow the uninitiated viewer to digest this information.

"And the affordable nature of technology these days, means that anyone with a very modest budget can create and distribute gonzo porn, without the problems of having film developed at Boots, where it would no doubt be seized, and you would be prosecuted and branded in our liberal media as a sick, twisted pervert, for looking at your own wife's , or husband's, bottom."

The slight tilt of David's head was because he got momentarily distracted wondering whether people still had any form of video or cine-film developed at Boots. He straightened his head again, not wanting to break from his current flow too much.

"Before the prurient brigade bemoan the lack of morals in today's degenerate society, this is not a moral or ethical change to people and their desires, as you might assume. Trust me, if your parents or grandparents could have made their own dirty movies in the privacy of their own homes, they would have jumped at the chance. Well, your grandfather would anyway, your grandmother would just have had to do as she was told, in that wonderful old-world way they had... unless she was a suffragette or lived in Bloomsbury, and in the latter case she'd have whipped them off at the drop of a deerstalker anyway... probably... and given the way society was behind closed doors a few decades ago, this imaginary historical home-porn would likely have been far more misogynistic and kinky than today's mainstream fare, but I feel myself digressing just a smidgeon..."

The 'Man in the Bath' allowed himself to slip under the water and gasped a breath when he came up, plastering his hair back over his forehead once more and wringing out the excess water, invigorated. He gave a little chuckle to himself. His own video could technically be described as porn, it was a naked man in the bath after all. He made a mental note to try and squeeze that observation in later.

"The point I was trying to make, before I got distracted by your grandmother, was that today, although it may not be admitted in polite society, more and more women are making adult movies themselves, and posting to 'what do you think' sites, where they receive positive, body affirming comments from sad little virgins, who are afraid to say anything negative in case the nudity stops happening. And a growing number of women are setting up home businesses, selling short video clips and 'softcore' porn to... well, let's be honest, quite literally, to wankers with more money than sense. So everyone is a winner in that respect. Even the prurient brigade win, as this gives them yet something else to complain about."

The Man in the Bath could feel himself drifting too far from the central conceit, and his voice took on a slightly sharper tone, annoyed at himself.

"The interesting thing is that the porn industry itself has taken to this trend like a duck to an English cricketer, and in equal amounts to the 'glossy, plastic, gyno-porn' it traditionally favoured, the industry is now creating FAKE 'gonzo' porn, with more realistic settings and body types. And here's the really interesting fact... this presents the feminists in the anti-porn camp with a small dilemma. On the one hand, they can't complain too much about the empowerment of women taking some control back from the commercial pornography industry, through choice and for their own profit, sisters 'doing it for themselves,' if you get my meaning."

The Man in the Bath burst out laughing, to his own surprise.

"...feel free to make your own innuendos from the last sentence... but back to the issue at hand. In addition to some women 'taking control' of the provision of erotica and pornography themselves on an amateur basis, even the mainstream, corporate providers have discovered tastes in the public domain have changed, and have started to deliver a more realistic portrayal, and I'm quite aware of how loose the term 'realistic' is here, of normal looking women rather than silicone sex dolls. Regardless of the camp who dislike the whole concept of porn, this recognition of a more natural and realistic body image promotion, has to be welcomed to at least some degree. So the argument now changes to the complaint and issue that society, primarily though not exclusively via the medium of pornography, is viewing 'real-looking' women as sexual objects. Not a new argument I know. But a flawed one IMHO, as we internet types say. That means 'in my humble opinion,' if you weren't sure, and this talk is just that, one man's humble opinion. But back to the subject. As a clarification, when I talk about 'porn,' I'm not just talking about money-shot movies. I'm talking about tease, nudity, erotica and literotica as well as shag-videos... anyway... "

The Man in the Bath paused, in what he hoped would be a 'what's coming next' moment of tension and anticipation. And to try and work out where he was going with all this, as he was currently in full-on improvisation mode.

"...anyway... sex objects... I hate to burst your bubble, boys and girls, but women *are* sexual objects to men. Just as men are sexual objects to women. And men to men, women to women, of course. But back to the point in hand."

Another grin. The British can find innuendo in almost anything.

"But this point, about us being sexual objects, is particularly true relating to other people who you don't know. If you have no interaction, knowledge of, or conversation with another person, then your only point of reference is what you physically see, making us all, quite literally, an object to a stranger's perspective. The urge to reproduce is quite old, you know, and the fact that I have sexual thoughts about women isn't necessarily a bad thing! It's a compliment, if you consider it objectively. It means you have all the right parts in the right places. Now, I'm not saying I base my whole world-view on sex, because I don't. A relationship is based on many more things than that, including that indefinable essence known as love, including respect, compatibility, appreciation, and communication, but that is talking about human interaction and relationships, rather than simply looking at someone you don't know. The fact that I want to fuck the girl next door has no bearing on my feelings for my partner, except perhaps for the rather important fact that I choose to stay with my partner and not do anything about the girl next door beside look, appreciate and occasionally think..."

He winked another 'never-to-be-seen behind the pixilation' wink.

"...no harm, no foul... and this is something I'm sure that the men out there will recognise and agree with, but which the female population, in the main, lack the self-confidence to accept as true, either about their partners, or themselves. I honestly believe that's all it is, a lack of self-confidence and trust in your partners... and before *you* get too cocky guys... it swings both ways... if you believe that argument about objectification yourself, then you can't, in all conscience, blame your other halves for fancying someone else either! Trust each other! Have faith! Repay that trust yourselves! But I'm wandering off the point, oh shit... I may edit all this bit out later ... too preachy... and slightly too much bollocks... one of my growing number of 'Dennis Norden' moments... or is he dead...? Might have to find another term if he is..."

A number of the videos, in their raw form, were interspersed with short interjections like this, where David just wandered that little bit too far off track, and got side-lined by unexpected questions. Sometimes, it led to wonderful new philosophies. Other times there were simply dead ends.

"...right, back to it, via a hopefully seamless edit... three, two, one... Likewise, I won't get into the whole area of prostitution or exploitation here, that's a separate issue in itself... for another time, my brethren... though one thing I do find fascinating is the media take on pornography... oh bollocks... there's too many routes to talk about here... this part is definitely for the out-takes show now... a little planning goes a long way!... remember that, David! When you're watching this back and cursing the hours of editing you're facing...oh... hang on... got it..."

He licked his lips, gathering thoughts into a cogent summing up moment, to be smoothly inserted. An apt turn of phrase he thought, amused at his own cleverness. Editing was a central part of his art now. Artificial technology was a godsend for faking natural rhythm.

"So is porn a feminist issue?'... let's look at the media... there's another relatively recent and pertinent phenomenon in terms of pornography, first popularised by that god-awful American Pie movie in the 1990's... that of the MILF... and for those of you unaware, or are lucky enough not to have seen the movie, it refers to, excuse the French... and the American... the 'Mom I'd Like to Fuck.' The concept isn't original of course, but in the porn world this term took off in a big way, hanging a label on a new niche market, and bringing 'porn respectability' to the many men in the world who find normal women sexually attractive, women who may have been married or had children, which is otherwise a bit of a taboo given the convoluted moral codes of the modern world. Well... putting everything else aside for just one moment, the promotion of post-teen women as objects of desire is nothing but good in my book, and a return, of ways, to the subjects of many wonderful paintings and portraits of past ages..."

David took a moment to further refine his direction. Practice and experience had shown that the best clips came from the sessions when he spoke in small, self-contained blocks of dialogue like this. Good for editing together. Good to make sure you didn't 'run out of steam.' That wasn't the problem this time though. Quite the opposite in fact. This topic really was too big for just one video.

"And this 'MILF' phenomenon caused a problem for the media, you see. The general acceptance of mothers and married women, as equally attractive to the twenty year old model, should be universally welcomed as a good thing. And is. It helps overcome some of the moral pressure that has exerted itself since Victorian times, that women cannot be seen as sexually attractive - except to their partners - once they are wed or bear children. But here's the crux of this problem. Members of the media - who obviously have no awareness of porn whatsoever!... obviously..."

Just the hint of a smile that he would have loved to have been visible came next. So he added a chuckle, to highlight the intended sarcasm audibly.

."..they recognised this as a good thing that society wanted, but couldn't overcome their commercial reliance on the PC lobby, and so could never countenance the promotion of the 'MILF' terminology and the words that created it... hence they invented, and please excuse me as I retch at the very term here, the alternate concept of the 'Yummy Mummy,' a rose by any other name. This controversy-friendly term has all the soft pronunciation and child-like rhyme sounds to be acceptable to the mass audience as non-offensive."

David paused one final time, and steepled his fingers in preparation for the imminent climax. To coin a phrase.

"... but the actual outcome of this is the de-sexualisation of the concept of wife and mother... she's nice, she's... 'pretty'... it's acceptable to call someone a 'yummy mummy'... after all... but you don't mean you actually want to fuck her, do you? That would be wrong."

That last was heavy with sarcastic conviction. David grinned, wishing there was a way that every single facial expression could be visible, to enhance the overall effect of these moments.

"Sometimes I do think... and it doesn't mean I will act on it, you understand... it doesn't mean I'll even try to... but yes... sometimes it's true, that I might want to fuck a particularly attractive woman who has had kids, just as much as I might want to fuck another attractive woman who hasn't... and that shouldn't be shocking! 'Is porn a feminist issue?' It should be. Sometimes, it tells the truth more than the mainstream... Man in the Bath... signing off."

David chuckled in delight, purely for himself this time. And yelled a comedy 'CUT!' for good measure. He tried to block out the uneasy deep-down sensation that the summing up had very little to do with the start, or the initial intention of the monologue. But he'd liked how the title sounded, so had wanted to let himself explore whatever his mind decided to throw out. David shrugged to no-one in particular. Didn't matter. He'd turn it back into something cogent and coherent with a few cuts and re-orderings. Find enough bits to make it relevant, and remove the parts that were total bollocks and couldn't be salvaged. The kernel would remain though. Controversial always got coverage and attention, whatever the actual content was. And this should ruffle some feathers.

Chp 8 – Revelations

He was quietly seething. The day had been going so well at first, not too many interruptions or stupid requests. He'd felt like he'd actually achieved some headway into the mountain of work. Then, David had come to the pub, as usual, for an after-work drink with the others; Saint, Nadine, Emily and Tyler, the usual suspects. He'd been in an excellent mood at the start. The week was over, most of the preparation work for the semester was done, and he'd previously been flirting with the rather attractive blonde barmaid with the big tits. Not even feeling guilty that she was ten years younger than he was. Okay, fifteen. Twenty.

It was in the middle of a discussion about a particular student (who had very unfortunately, and quite amusingly, laughed so hard during a tutorial that she'd wet herself), that he'd caught a snippet of conversation from two girls at the next table. And his attention had been immediately drawn.

"...and he calls himself the 'Man in the Bath'... it's hilarious."

"Really?"

"Oh yes. He obviously thinks he's got all these great and wonderful philosophical thoughts... but basically, he's just a dick with a chip on his shoulder. He's making a total nob of himself, and he hasn't got a clue."

"Is he fit?"

A rather evil giggle followed.

"You clearly haven't seen it, or you wouldn't have to ask. He's a flabby, pasty, middle-aged bloke, with saggy man-boobs."

David tried hard to focus back on the conversation at his own table, desperately willing himself not to blush with embarrassment and shame. At the same time he urgently wanted to hear more. Even if it was bad, he was being talked about. And that was always interesting. He lifted his glass to appear nonchalant and disinterested, and pondered with a little self-revelation, that it was only the 'middle aged' part of the description that actually stung.

"He obviously can't get any, as half of the clips are really nasty, anti-women bitch-fests, and it's not surprising looking at him."

David chanced a look out of the corner of his eye and was surprised to see the conversation was between two female students that he vaguely knew. They were from a different department but had both taken modules in Critical Theory before. He'd always thought they were rather nice.

"What does he look like then?"

Another giggle.

"Probably grotesque, because he blurs his face out so you can't see it. He's probably hideous and does it so the people watching won't throw up. AND he's got a pony tail! At his age! I bet he's bald on top. You can tell, now and then, when he hasn't disguised it properly. Ewww!"

It was only then that David realised he was staring directly at the girls. And a moment too late when he realised that they were both looking right back at him.

"Hi, Dr Dunn."

David couldn't stop himself from blushing then, blushing and being intensely aware of the length and receding tendencies of his own hair.

"Hello Michelle... errr... Sophie..."

He turned back quickly in embarrassment, just catching the whispered giggle of "Oh God, do you think he heard us? HE's got a pony tail too!" David looked up and caught a couple of odd glances from his fellow drinkers. He leaned in to the group of lecturers.

"Better be careful what we say... those two are our students."

Emily nodded, and reluctantly switched the conversation away from a discussion of her more amusing tutees, and onto where they would go to eat. David absently threw in a suggestion of the vegetarian restaurant by the canal, as he tried to catch any further insights or comments from the next table. Unfortunately, the subject there had changed as well.

And it was at this exact point in time that, for the first time, the epiphany hit Dr David Dunn that people must have been looking at his website. And if a student from his own University had seen it, the chances were that a lot more people had, elsewhere. Either that, or what he'd just overheard was the biggest co-incidence ever. He nodded in agreement to a suggestion of a pub meal, and had to almost physically stop himself from turning round and asking where the student Sophie had heard about the Man in the Bath.

David's next thought was to head straight home and Google himself on the internet. The subsequent thought to that, was that he should take the website down immediately. And that particular thought hit him like a lorry. He was a laughing stock. The one thing Dr David Dunn didn't deal with well, was humiliation.

He had to reluctantly drag himself back to the conversation at his own table, as he realised Nadine was staring at him with raised eyebrows.

"You okay, Dave?"

He nodded absently, trying to force all the worrying and conflicting possible consequences out of his racing mind, and away from his facial expression.

"Just thinking."

"You don't want to do that. Bad for the health, thinking! Just focus on something pleasant and distracting."

Dr Nadine Silk leaned forwards slightly over the table, smirking wickedly as she revealed a flash of cleavage, down her V-neck top. David smiled weakly back. Normally that would have been a very pleasant and effective distraction, and would have led to another bout of harmless, covert flirting. Right now it was just an annoying distraction. He took out his mobile phone and pretended to read a message to break the contact. It seemed to work, as he heard a distinctly unsatisfied harrumph from across the table.

That was when he started to get annoyed, his attention elsewhere once more. All his hard work had been for nothing. It didn't matter that they'd sneered at his physical form, but if that was all the reaction his recordings were going to get...

David's nose wrinkled, his mouth contorting as though he had an unpleasant taste there. The point of it had always been the words and the world-view. He was stupid for thinking people would see past the physical.

The anger started to point inwards at his own lack of forethought in such an obvious outcome. The anger started to grow. David wasn't aware of the odd glances he was receiving from the corner of Nadine's eye.

Chp 9 – Google

He typed 'Man in the Bath' into the search engine and paused, sipping his Rioja and soda water, and drawing in a deep breath. It was a blasphemy of a drink in public, but in private David quite liked it. Closing his eyes, he hit 'enter.' He wasn't quite sure why, but felt very nervous and could feel his cheeks were burning up, even though he was quite alone. Humiliation awaited. Or hopefully nothing, no trace of the search term. That would be the preferable outcome at this juncture. David was holding his breath as his eyes re-opened. A page appeared filled with the highlighted search phrase.

He started to click through the results, gulping a little heavily at the wine. The first result re-enforced all of the worst fears. It was a messageboard forum, taking the piss out of the 'Man in the Bath' website. And suggesting that anyone reading the messages should not even bother looking up the 'ugly, fascist, sexist pig' himself. Strangely, that relaxed, rather than angered, him. It was more of a relief than anything else. At least now, he knew what to expect. Even knowing the worst was better than not knowing at all.

The next result was more of a surprise, and brought a satisfied exhalation and upwards curl of the lips. It pointed to the website again, but this time, told surfers that they'd find it really funny. And the post wasn't at all disparaging, just amused. The third result was the site itself. And that surprised the most of all. David wasn't an expert on search engines by any means, but such a high ranking in the results meant that he had been getting a large number of hits; he was fairly sure of that. He kept scrolling down and further down, growing increasingly amazed and not a little self-satisfied, as result after result referred to his site, and the vast majority in complimentary or positive terms. Finally, bored of reading similar comments, he clicked on one of the links to his own site. And found nothing. Nothing but a 'bandwidth exceeded' message.

The administrator dashboard for the website showed why. Four thousand hits in the last week alone. David Dunn was staggered. It was like being physically punched and the sensation left him panting for breath. He got up, leaving the statistic on the screen, and headed for the fridge to get himself a beer. Then changed his mind and fetched a bottle of scotch from the cupboard where he kept the hoover. A special 12 year old single malt which he'd been saving for an unspecified 'occasion.'

After the second straight whisky, gulped while standing in the hall, he sat back at the computer and, to the strains of an Ali Farke Touré CD, adjusted the settings. The advantage of administering your own website was that you could adjust the bandwidth allocated at the click of a mouse. Within five minutes, the site was live once more and David was at the messageboard, noting with satisfaction that three 'guests' had logged on within ten minutes of the site becoming available, and noting that he now had over six hundred 'registered' members, despite the fact that this conferred no special privileges or advantages. David hadn't even thought about extra features you could provide on the internet. The memberships and the messageboards were part of the default website template he'd used. Apart from a title page and the clips, he hadn't added any other content at all. It was time to have a proper look at what was going on.

David was still sitting at his computer screen scrolling through the messages at half-past eleven, by now quite definitely drunk. The missives people had left on various discussion and review sites varied considerably, but the vast majority were still positive, with several threads taking individual 'Man in the Bath' episodes (there were now fifteen, a mixture of the old, original ones and the more recently created), and either deconstructing, or expanding on them. He fumbled for a pen and jotted a quick note to himself for the morning, to arrange the site layout better, and allow people the chance to comment more easily on particular subjects or posts. Then he returned to one of several earnest questions that had been left on his own site, and jotted a few more notes on how he should answer, something sensible inside warning that answering drunk might be a mistake.

Squinting a little, David searched his hard drive for one of the as-yet unused video files, and ran it through once to ensure it had already been fully edited to remove any nudity. There was a strange kind of pride resonating round his shoulders, possibly enhanced by the whisky, as he attached the saved title sequence and hit 'upload.'

Switching the media player to select the strains of Snoop Dog and Limp Bizkit, he nodded his head and carefully typed a message onto the comments section of his site under a nickname of 'The Administrator.'

'Thank you all for your comments. I'm happy to have provoked a reaction where I have, and that you've found my words of interest or in some cases of comfort. I'm uploading my thoughts on 'The Church' for you now, as I seem to have built one of my own. Now, I don't mean to offend anyone but...'

He paused, then pressed delete to remove the last word. Then pressed it again until he'd removed the last sentence in its entirety.

It's what I felt at the time of recording. If you don't agree, then you don't agree. Feel free to say so. That is your right, just as it is my right to say what I feel. Discuss, comment, do what you feel but please try to stick to the subject of the individual videos where you can, and be kind to other posters. They have a right to their opinions too, even if you disagree. Soon I will gift to you all, my two-minute guide to enlightenment!'

He grinned at the last sentence and lifted up the bottle, the liquid now below the level of the label, toasting the screen.

#

By half-past two in the morning, David was almost sober again, but was still sitting at the computer table, this time on the desktop PC where he did his more 'serious' work, and was typing a direct personal reply to a young woman who had confided a secret to the messageboard. It was a short reply, as comforting as he could make it, though it still sounded very twee to his own ears. He added a suggestion that she e-mail him directly at the administrator address on the site. There was a warm sensation to be had doing that. And that wasn't just the after effects of the wine and whisky. If no-one else treated his website as anything more than a joke, then at least this one person had seen something in him and wanted to confide. That felt good. That felt nice. Cracking his knuckles, David started to type a draft response e-mail. He decided that he already knew the advice he'd give, so he may as well write it now, while he remembered. When the woman contacted him, which she surely would, he could tweak the draft with any personal details she might mention. Such as the actual nature of her problem.

Chp 10 – Enlightenment

The next day seemed to go on forever. It was 'options-choice' time for the students, and that meant most of David's day would be taken up with e-mails, phone calls, and personal visits from students and lecturers, wanting reminding of the rules, or to find out where they could access information. At one point, he almost recorded a short speech into a Dictaphone to leave outside the door, directing people to read the instructions on the noticeboards or to *read their fucking e-mails* but instead, as usual, he wore the pained smile and, whilst being (mostly) polite, repeated the same instructions over and over again, to a succession of visitors.

The only exception to the frustration came on account of one particular girl from the third year, who David always struggled with. She was a Spanish exchange student ,with short, dark curly hair and an impressive chest that made him stumble over his words, and she had proved a very welcome distraction. This distraction had been followed as usual by a fleeting period of silent self-recrimination and wishes that the 'old University' ways were still in place, so that he could safely abuse his position in all the ways she made him think about.

But for most of the day, David simply just waited to go home. That was the main driving force. He still resisted the urge to check his own website at work, but spent every second in public, in the café, and in the student bar, hoping to catch a mention of the 'Man in the Bath' in someone else's conversation. Without luck.

A further plan did emerge though. While it was beneficial and easy to use the University website for his little videos (the server masked by the little trick he knew), it wasn't very safe, and eventually someone would notice, particularly now that the number of visitors was so high. He was careful enough to be certain that the method he'd used would avoid all but the most direct investigation, but it was time to buy some personal webspace proper. Or he *would* be discovered. It was sod's law. David made a mental note to google the phrase 'sod's law' when he got home. It might have an interesting etymology.

#

David's girlfriend telephoned at half-past eleven, just before lunch, and the content of that conversation came as a bit of a shock. Liz worked in Bath now, quite appositely, and had spent the previous two months in Washington DC, negotiating contracts with a large American conglomerate. He hadn't even realised she'd been gone for most of the time.

As soon as David put the phone down after that call, it rang again. He just let the sound continue. It had never been what you'd have called a serious relationship in terms of commitment, but they *had* been together for almost three years. Together on paper, at least. In practical terms, it was phone calls, a weekend, or a bank holiday here or there, and a fortnight in the Seychelles, the year before last. Plus sex, whenever the subject or opportunity arose. Given the fact neither of them owned a car, and Leeds was a four-hour train ride from Bath, hadn't occurred with great frequency.

David wasn't particularly surprised that Liz had found someone else that she'd rather be with, although an intercontinental 'Dear John' of less than five minutes duration was a little disappointing. In a natural temper, mainly that she'd been the one to do the dumping, he'd highlighted this disappointment in a very pointed way, as being a sign of her insensitivity. Liz had answered in an equally defensive tone that a disappointing five minutes from a distant partner seemed quite a fitting way to end the relationship. David ignored the knock at the door, getting up as silently as he could to turn the key, and lock the door from the inside. He berated his eyes as they started to water, probably because of the pollen, drifting through the open window.

#

One hour, and one pleading e-mail later, and David was sitting with Nadine in a backstreet Italian restaurant explaining, in a slightly shell-shocked way, that he'd been dumped. It was by only saying it out loud that the consequences really took precedence over the manner of the break-up. Nadine looked uncomfortable at the news, and pulled her jacket closed across her chest.

"It's not that unexpected, is it? You hardly ever see her, hardly ever mention her..."

Dave sucked air in through his teeth, trying to appear calm and ignoring the shaking inside.

"I know that. I'd just hoped that when it finally ended, it would at least be face-to-face so..."

"So you'd get a consolation shag?"

He blushed and tried not to smirk at the unfortunately accurate question, failing completely. Nadine had an uncanny knack of pointing out the unstated when he didn't want her to. And of bringing the conversation back to a more palatable level.

"Not just that!"

"And you asked me here... because?"

His nose wrinkled, and then a little light went on, somewhere in his brain.

"Oh, I don't want to fuck you, that's not it..."

"You don't?"

It was Nadine's turn to look slightly amused now. Amused, relieved, and disbelieving, all at the same time. That made Dave grin a little more, and relax a fraction, himself.

"Okay. I do. Of course, I do. But that isn't why I brought you here. I just wanted to get it off my chest... and maybe look at yours, while I did to take my mind off... what was her name again?"

His eyeline slid downwards as the sentence tailed off, to illustrate the points. It was obviously the right thing to say, and the humour and admission, perversely seemed to make Nadine more comfortable too. She knew him well enough by now to know that if his real intention was seduction, he'd be far more devious about it, and embarrassed about being caught out. She loosened the jacket.

"Go on then. Perv away. And tell me you're really that bothered."

Dave pouted. Nadine really did know him too well. And well enough to know that his eyes wouldn't need to leave her face any more today, now that they had permission. He also knew that now they'd fallen into the flirtation routine, he couldn't go on to admit the genuine depth of his hurt feelings either. But it could take his mind off the dull ache that was starting.

"You know I'm not bothered. It was just a bit of a shock. Always is, getting dumped, isn't it?"

"How would I know?"

Dave resisted the urge to stick out his tongue. He felt juvenile whenever they had chats like this.

"Well, it is. And I didn't like the way that she did it."

"Have you cheated on her while she's been away?"

"Only in my head."

"Because you didn't want to, or because you didn't get the chance?"

"You're far too perceptive to be this attractive, you know!"

She smiled coyly and crossed her legs, leaning forwards to lean on her palm, elbow on the table, mirroring David's own pose.

"Did you cheat with me... in your head?"

His eyes narrowed deliberately in response.

"Only once. And only for the articles."

"Only once? I must be losing my touch. Who did you think about cheating with for real? The barmaid in The Swan? That Spanish student?"

"I thought you were meant to be sympathising with me?"

Nadine batted her eyelashes coquettishly.

"You prefer this..."

Chp 11 – Changing Your Provider

It was eight pm by the time David reached his house. The afternoon had been very wearing, full of the usual annoyances, and had been made even more frustrating by the fact that lunch with Nadine had been over too quickly. The resurfacing and persistent memories of being dumped played a part in affecting is mood too, and of it having taken place by phone.

David hadn't even thought about looking at the website since the dumping though so, after a bolted microwave special fried rice, he settled down in front of the big computer and started by quickly searching for new web-hosting services. He needed something further to occupy his obsessive mind. Prices seemed very reasonable and, within the hour, he'd redirected the URL and was uploading the entire site to the new web-space, blanking out everything but the work at hand. He was starting to enjoy himself with the methodical detail of the task, and forget the other troubles. David paid more than the usual amount of attention to ensuring all that traces of the previous site were wiped from the University servers. Better safe than sorry.

A bottle of beer was tonight's sustenance as David started to surf through the messages, surprised to find quite a number of eager acolytes, almost begging for the guide to enlightenment which he'd recently promised. This was a slight issue, as he didn't have one. It had been a spur of the moment reference, which felt good at the time, but no such video existed.

Memories of Liz kept encroaching unexpectedly, along with other unpleasant thoughts of a more job-related nature, and David read the comments quickly, trying to find something suitably intriguing to fully occupy his whole brain. Surprisingly, it came on the thread relating to the pornography and women rant, from a woman going under the moniker of 'Barechested_princess.'

Thank you for what you said about pornography and feminism. I know that may sound strange coming from a mother, but I've read your other pieces too, and I think I understand what you're saying. You also replied personally to a friend of mine, and what you said was really kind, and helped her a lot. I don't want to say any more on here so I'll send you an e-mail to the admin address. I'll put my username in the title.

This was intriguing enough to stop any other lingering memories of Liz, and David settled back, trying to guess which of the two personal replies he'd sent so far could have been to the friend in question. And while his mind span over that little query, he absently made a slight alteration to the site, putting a warning up on the front page that "although 'The Man in the Bath' would eventually read all e-mails, there were too many for him to be able to reply to every one, and he couldn't guarantee a personal response." And that he was sorry.

David deleted the part about being sorry. You had to be firm about these things. Although he wasn't swamped yet (two direct messages was hardly being swamped), he didn't want to set a precedent by promising he'd have to give an answer on any old shit. It was a lesson he'd learned early in his career at the University. The first months in the job had been terrible, as he'd tried to help every single student and staff member who'd come to him with an issue or a conundrum. His workload was just about manageable now that he selected only the important things. Back then, it had been an extra three or four hours every night, and working half the weekend or more, just to keep from falling any further behind.

There were already seven e-mails to 'The Administrator' today, which vindicated the new disclaimer, and David perversely looked through the other six unexpected unknown senders first. Three were abuse, and he summarily blocked and banned the culprits. Two were personal requests for the 'enlightenment piece,' and one was a serious but polite question about his thoughts on gay marriage, explaining that the inclusion of this in a future video could help stimulate discussion in the 'Community,' as it was a personal moral issue to the poster.

He paused, and re-read the final request. The syntax, from an obviously eloquent sender, suggested that the 'Community' in question was made up from the members of his site. That brought a satisfied smile, a hint of pride, and a slightly patronising reply. He thanked the sender for the idea and suggested that he ask around 'the Community' himself first, to see if anyone else would be interested. David added a little coda explaining that he would ask himself, but wanted a more objective opinion, knowing that anything he offered would be taken up by his viewers.

He hit 'send' and fetched another beer, before turning his attention to the 'Barechested_princess' message. And then flushed, and felt a little uncomfortable when he read what she'd written.

I know that some of what you write is provocative, but you seem to understand women, even if you try and hide it behind humour and provocation. What you wrote to my friend (pixie_FC) was exactly what she needed to hear, and she seemed to take notice of your advice, but you wrote so beautifully and sensitively too.

Dave racked his brain to try and imagine what wondrous insights he'd given, but only remembered a very twee and clichéd drunken e-mail sympathising, and suggesting the woman start by taking a step back from her emotions to write down the real problems on a piece of paper, and cross out all those she had the power to solve herself. All he could think of at the time. Not rocket science, and not very insightful, but it had sufficed.

You'll be glad to know she seems much better now, and your suggestion helped her put her real problems into perspective. But that's not the reason I'm writing. It's rare to find a man so attuned to women and I'm guessing that all you get from the website is people with problems wanting advice. That isn't me. I just want to fuck you.

That sentence was re-read five or six times before he moved on. A new mixture of pride, lust, fear, and pity, swirled in his belly. The rest of the e-mail was just a phone number and a picture of an attractive brunette in her thirties, smiling with a glass of wine in her hand at some bar. Quite proper. Fully dressed. And then an odd postscript.

I'd really like to do it in your bath. You don't have to post the video. And you don't have to give me a copy. No strings. xxx

More beer was drunk as David digested the e-mail several times over, slowly, from start to finish. And then he got up to do something else. Anything else. And in the circumstances, a walk to the off-license seemed the most appropriate 'anything else.'

#

Having thought through the offer and its implications from every conceivable angle, David found himself perversely focusing on the part that said his message had helped 'pixie_FC.' Common sense had seemingly been all that was needed. And now, consequently, he was apparently being seen as some kind of real guru. He hadn't been back onto the site yet, and didn't want to until he had decided what to do. Without thinking, David started to type into a blank Word document, and within 30 minutes, the piece had evolved into the elusive guide to enlightenment that had been promised. Incorporating what he thought was a modicum of common sense.

He read through it to check for consistency and spelling, half-pleased, and half-wondering exactly how much of this sort of crap he could possibly get away with. Nodding to himself (and now swaying slightly), David decided that it would be a good test of 'the Community.' It would help him identify the total nutters from the followers who were truly worth conversing with.

Blinking at the keyboard, he concentrated on his fingers as he turned his attention to typing a reply for the 'princess,' thanking her but asking her not to offer again. Full of his own importance, David typed that while he was obviously flattered, he didn't want to take advantage of anyone he was offering advice to, and that wasn't why he made the videos or hosted the site. He couldn't resist joking at the end, a little comment about how he'd liked the idea of a video of someone else in the bath for a change. Though her suggestion of the content might not fit in with the tone of the rest of the site.

He wouldn't have written anything like that if he'd been sober, but the alcohol and offer of sex were acting as a little devil on his shoulder. The suspicion that it might have been a wind-up had disappeared along with the alcohol, over the course of the evening. Sighing heavily, David posted the reply without reviewing it, then moved to upload the latest document, the guide to enlightenment. It had wandered off a bit in places, but that was only because he'd started to enjoy himself and allowed his words to run away in whatever direction they preferred. Some of the facts might be dubious, but no-one would bother too much about that. It was the thought that counted, as the saying went. This one wasn't a video from the bath, but they'd just have to make do with a written copy of his plan for enlightenment. Anyway, he wanted to put a picture in it, with captions and a legend, and everything associated. He couldn't do pictures if he was talking on video. David had been immensely proud of the little associated diagram he'd created, and hadn't yet noticed that he'd deleted it by accident about fifteen minutes earlier.

He got up, and staggered sideways into the occasional table. Holding himself upright, David looked down at the phone, and thought about Liz in America. Unreachable. About Nadine at home.

Unavailable. And about the bare-chested princess…

He forced himself, with difficulty, to move towards the bedroom and avoid the temptation to go back and send a quite different e-mail reply. He'd find another way to deal with those thoughts.

Chp 12 – 5 Minute Guide to Enlightenment (written)

A number of you have asked, so here it is. Written down so that you can print it out to read and digest wherever you feel the most comfortable (careful not to get the pages wet if you choose the bath!). Now, let me explain some fundamental constants, and introduce you to the basic truths of, and path to, enlightenment...

<u>The Background</u>

The basic tenets of Nirvanah, or Enlightenment, are present in most belief systems, but the 'path' varies according to doctrine or, very occasionally, common sense. The basis is the perception of 'self' in relation to the world, and is about your self-awareness. It is best described in a similar fashion to a gyroscope, as it should really show movement, but that's getting into the realms of advanced enlightenment, and you're a novice. I also wanted to mention gyroscopes as they are wonderful inventions, they represent the laws of physics, reflect spiritual 'one-ness,' and are fun to play with too ☺

The Celtic 'Dyfalu' poetic principle of the 'wandering and enclosing line' is also useful in understanding, as it can be used to reflect and envelope the concept of the soul/ spirit/ the 'id' (to get Freudian and secular on your ass for a moment), which is part of the world and the universe, tied to, but also apart from, it. 'Dyfalu' is also the basis for my rather natty tattoo, which you may have spotted in my videos. Don't let the depth and complexities of the 'Dyfalu' pattern confuse you further with what is already a very muddy concept of enlightenment, but I think it's a useful way to reflect on the malleability and journey of the path to enlightenment. Anything spiritual and non-corporeal is likely to be confusing; just go with the flow for now my friends.

I find it amusing that the literal translation of 'Dyfalu' is 'guesswork,' which fits my thesis here too. Let's get back to the journey towards enlightenment in simple terms though, and invent points 'A', 'B' and 'C' at equal points around an imaginary circle, to represent different points on the path to awareness, and let us call this circle, for the sake of argument, 'the self.'

<u>The fundamental problem</u>
There are incredibly good hints and backgrounds put forward by most spiritual or religious movements, and all the 'great faiths,' but there is a particularly good and

simple background in a book by a bloke called Suzuki, on the concepts of Zen (I forget what the book is called) if you would like to read further. Zen is an excellent and exceedingly popular 'path,' as it does not preclude a God/ gods, which probably accounts for its popularity across a broad spectrum of truth seekers. You can be Christian, Taoist, Zoroastrionist, any old shit, and still be a Zen 'Buddhist' (which is a very vague and slightly inaccurate term, but it's popular, so I'll appropriate it). Their path to enlightenment accepts that individual beliefs and experience do not exclude, or necessitate, an actual faith. It is self-awareness that leads to enlightenment, and this is apart from formal religion. A fundamental of 'self-awareness' is that it can't be taught though, by definition, it must come from within the self. While faith can assist some people in this, it must ultimately be a personal discovery and choice (which is where you get into the Pelagian heresy and shit like that, which is v interesting but a different issue. Pelagius rocks by the way!). The difficulty that most 'paths' have in guiding to enlightenment, is that by instructing people, you intrinsically influence and therefore alter them, making the true 'self awareness' more difficult. It's a Catch 22. It's tied in to the whole 'nature vs nurture' debate of true individuality and growth. Anyway, this is one of the reasons that the zen 'path' often uses obscure methods like haiku poetry and Confucian riddles, to instruct followers, as these distractions make people work meaning out for themselves. There's an interesting parallel with people who self harm, strangely, but again that is a separate issue. Basically, zen just says that you cannot really 'teach' enlightenment. I think that's bollocks. It just means it is difficult, and takes a good teacher. Like me.

<u>The bones of it</u>

Anyway, the underlying fact is that people begin at point 'A' on our imaginary circle of self; think of an archery target, and we're on the red ring halfway in, with our perception of the Universe all around us (the outer blue circle), and the reality of some undefined universal 'truth' as the golden bullseye in the middle. Got that picture in your head? At this point, human nature leads people to search for 'the answer,' 'truth,' 'the path,' or some crap like that, and how someone can physically reach the golden circle at the centre of life, where they think they will discover the answer to everything. They want to move their 'self' from the red middle ring we're currently on, to this magic panacea of the golden bullseye. As people search for a way to access the universal truth, this 'Nirvanah,' they move around the red ring, figuratively speaking, trying diverse ways to seek and find enlightenment, looking for different angles on their life, looking for solutions, and searching for that route to the golden bullseye that solves all of life's problems. With me so far, my brethren?

This moves us to point 'B' on the red ring of 'self,' about a third of the way round the circumference, as we've started looking for a different way to access our golden bullseye of the answer to everything, and we've done this by making changes to our own lives, and outlooks. We haven't found a route into the middle ring yet, but we are now looking towards the centre (and our ultimate objective) from a different part of the red 'self' ring, so we have a different perspective on life. This movement from 'A' to 'B' represents changes people may make within themselves (attitudes, beliefs, 'looking at the world differently' etc) which they see as development, personal growth, or progress towards their ultimate enlightenment.

Thinking they're making progress, the acolyte carries on making further changes to their own lifestyle and thinking, and this moves us further around the circumference of the red ring, to reach point 'C,' now progressing to two thirds of the way around the circle. From this new viewpoint, people may feel they have changed within themselves, and be almost diametrically opposed to where they felt they were, when they first started this journey of discovery. They could well be at the farthest point from how they felt, and acted, at the beginning, but they are still both 'within' the red ring of 'self,' looking towards the unachievable golden bullseye of perfect enlightenment, and are still surrounded by the same blue ring of the universe, existence, and all the pressures and influence of the wider world.

Some seekers of the truth may move to point 'B' or 'C' in their journey of self-discovery and may stop at one of those points, happier with the slightly different view of the world, or believing they have 'developed' enough. That can be its own reward.

The concept of true enlightenment though, is when you have explored all aspects of the 'self,' and move all the way round the red to arrive right back at point 'A' once again. In one way, it is true that you are back where you were at the very beginning. The difference is that, having completed your search for a pathway to the bullseye of perfection, and found there is no such thing, you are able to accept that there is no 'Answer,' or ultimate solution, to the difficulties in your life. There is no way to access the bullseye of perceived perfection. Instead, you just accept the reality of your life as it is, the good and the bad, and that the journey was more important than the destination.

As this whole imaginary gold, red and blue target represents the larger view of the broader 'self,' once you've explored every angle, you realise you can never escape your place halfway to the centre, that there will always be a gold 'perfection' which can never be reached, and always a blue layer around you, the universe with all its complexity and pressure and unavoidable and unpredictable nature. You can never *change that, as this would mean a change to the physical, which is separate to the spiritual.*

The three imaginary rings are also in perpetual motion, as time itself moves on, and it is this constant rotation (as in a gyroscope), which means that a fixed route towards total enlightenment could never exist, and even your best efforts towards perfection can never end. The 'gravitational path' of existence is truly inescapable.

So the best result to the search for enlightenment is reaching the point at which you've travelled the whole circumference of the red ring of self, and realise, and finally accept, that your life is simply what it is, and that there is no route to a magic solution for all of your problems in life.

You can still strive to improve and change for the better, but you are no longer looking for the elusive and non-existent 'answer to everything' (which would mean you had transcended humanity Siddhartha style, at which point the religious ones (Buddhists aside) would be truly buggered as it would make them a 'god.') This is why the Stoics were so highly rated by earlier Christian movements as they had achieved the doctrinal Christian version of Nirvanah. It's also the basis for the age old 'prayer' which occurs in some form in most religions, the 'give me the ability to change what I can, the strength to accept what I cannot change, and the wisdom to know the difference' one.

So, to sum up, enlightenment is a self awareness of reality and the true and wholehearted internal ability to accept that sometimes, there are no perfect answers or solutions which can come from the outside, only your own ability to change yourself. Any guidance you receive to help towards spiritual enlightenment is not a solution, merely a pointer in the direction you need to look within yourself. It should be used, like religion, only as a crutch when needed, and, to carry on the analogy, when your broken leg is healed, you shouldn't keep using crutches. Or your own legs will weaken from non-use.
Be honest and true to yourself only, my children.
Forward through perspective and introspection!
There endeth the lesson.

 I hope you feel duly enlightened

The Man in the Bath™

Chp 13 – Copycat

The next day was all sorts of bizarre. David resisted the strong urge to check on his website first thing in the morning, and had walked into University totally focused on his actual work. After a shower, three strong sugary coffees and four paracetamol, that is. At eleven am he picked up an answerphone message from Liz, apologising for the day before, and asking to meet up with him when she came back for a visit in November (her trip had been extended).

Professor Furber arrived in his room at twelve, bizarrely trying to persuade David to take part in what could only be described as a pyramid scheme.

At lunch in the pub Nadine ignored him completely, so David ate his sandwich quickly, and left for the internet café (with the mantra 'don't look at the website at work, it leaves an audit trail'), to check the messageboards, ignoring his previous resolution to have a 'MITB'-free day.

The 'Community' had apparently been engaged in a lively debate on the concept of gay marriage in relation to religious dogma. So he added a pompous declaration from the

Administrator, that he was happy this subject was being tackled by everyone without his help. And that he wouldn't be adding his own personal thoughts, which were only ever meant as a starting point to spark debate and conversation. He was satisfied that the 'Community' was working for itself on this matter.

There was an e-mail from Barechested_princess which was short, to the point, and occupied his mind for the rest of the day. There was no address or subject line.

In answer to your reasoning... It wouldn't be taking advantage, so yes, you could. A number of us have discussed it in the private chatroom and just so you know, I'm not the only one who wants you.
No pressure though.
I understand and respect your decisions and reasons. The offer remains open. As elected spokesperson, I have to say that the willingness and desire for you apply to a number of us, but if you change your mind, I hope that you'll think of me first. I'm not jealous, you can have as many of us as you please, but I want to be the first.
I'd still like to send you a video of myself. I know it wouldn't be appropriate for the website, I meant just for you. To tell you what my thoughts are on you. And show you. I can do it from the bath if you'd like, though on

reflection I'd prefer to do it from my bed, because that's where I think about you the most. Please may I send it?

David was late back for work, and smelling of whisky, as he turned the peculiar message over and over in his head. It wasn't just peculiar, it was actually unbelievable, in the literal sense. It must be a wind-up, as that was the most unrealistic email a real woman would ever send. But she talked about 'the Community' too. And it was so peculiar and unbelievable, that it didn't seem like anything someone could make up and send. Perversely, its weirdness suggested to David that the message and offer must be genuine. Although possibly from a lunatic. His head told him to break contact with the woman instantly. The rest of him was tempted, despite his misgivings. His head continued to debate with his body's baser instincts, to limited success.

This had been a totally unexpected development and needed some detailed thought on a more objective and philosophical level. He was being offered what he could only assume was a pornographic home movie, from a woman he didn't know, because he videoed his own quite unexceptional views on life. Offered in a very polite and insistent way. The use of the submissive

'Please may I?' in particular, seemed disturbingly appealing.

A whole internal dialogue on the matter had already taken place while David had been drinking the whisky, about the possible motivations of the woman, her mental health, who she was, and on a baser level, if he should take advantage of the offer, now that he was genuinely single. Not that being single mattered to David greatly, but the confluence of events was fortuitous. His mind had stayed on the subject even as he'd returned to the office.

The germ of an evil thought floated around his skull repeatedly, along with a half-remembered quote from Ron Hubbard about starting a religion. He couldn't help chuckling at the fact that this little hobby already seemed to have earned him acolytes and groupies, without any particular effort, and David absently wondered if the money would follow Which, in turn, prompted intermittent daydreams of chat show appearances and a mansion with a pool, playing Beatles records from an expensive stereo. Cruder visions also occurred, picturing what the other women of the Community might look like, the ones that the Barechested princess had suggested he could 'have' if he wanted to. He could help pondering if he might know any of them in real life.

David mechanically opened the mail. There was a letter detailing two training courses he was booked on, a letter from the pensions company about an error on his account, three complaints about University procedure from parents, and six bills. Sighing, he put them in the physical in-tray for later and dialled the automated system to pick up his voicemail messages, before tackling the in-box of the electronic mail. The fact that all his subconscious wanted was to hear Liz's voice to drag him back towards reality never came close to invading his surface thoughts.

#

The general departmental meetings were usually a welcome diversion, and if nothing else, were always entertaining. This was the regular open meeting when staff members could discuss current issues, matters of policy, gossip, and generally moan in an official capacity. It was greatly enjoyed by all, in part, because it was one of the few meetings when modern legislation didn't require a student representative, or the taking of minutes. This meant that the veneer of the professional academic could be dropped, and true natures could come out. Students could be mocked and derided for their ignorance and stupidity quite openly. The same applied to absent colleagues.

David had eventually managed to force his full concentration back to the meeting, and was currently influencing the direction of a syllabus-based decision in the way he enjoyed most. Nadine was smirking in his general direction. After the last of these meetings, she'd whispered that her new name for him was 'puppet master.' She was always discreet enough not to mention it in front of other colleagues, but was perceptive enough to recognise how he played certain members of the academic fraternity. While the Saint and Professor Cornwell were mid-flow on the lack of general interest that Liberal Arts students seemed to have in reading, David threw in a light comment about having some sympathy, and how they could hardly *enforce reading in student's spare time*, deliberately catching the eyes of one of the more vociferous academics at the last statement. Nadine's eyes twinkled, watching him carefully, as the reverse psychology paid off, just as expected. The throwaway comment was taken up, and expanded seriously, which of course had been the intention all along. It seemed that the concept of reverse psychology was as alien to some academics as good grammar seemed to be to some of the students. With certain specific individuals, knowing that David was against something was reason enough for fight for it. He desperately wanted to tell some of them how easy they were to manipulate, but that would ruin the process. Maybe he'd save it for his memoirs.

Elias interjected at that point. In a strange leap of logic, he somehow managed to comment on the loudness of adverts on television, and made this sound relevant. The long, silver hair slipped from behind his ear and over his specs, as he enthusiastically inserted one of those many facts he seemed to pluck from no-where, on the percentage louder that adverts were legally allowed to be, compared to actual television programmes (and the exact number of times this rule had been broken in the last three months). Everyone listened when Elias spoke in these meetings. Partly because he always seemed to know the oddest facts, often pertaining to popular culture, something that seemed totally against the entire nature of Elias, but mainly because no-one was ever quite sure how he fitted these interjections in so seamlessly, when they were completely irrelevant to the subject in hand. Elias' brain was an enigma to them all. He was a gifted teacher and amazing font of knowledge (that much was universally agreed), but he seemed even more abstract to reality, social graces, and conversation than the most hardened of the other academics.

Normally David loved these moments himself, but today he just felt frustrated. He was trying to implement a specific policy, and this sidebar was pulling people away from the smooth introduction of his 'credits for additional reading' programme.

Barechested_Princess squeezed herself into his brain without warning. It was as though his head had decided, if distractions were allowed, then he'd return to his own best pre-occupations.

"Did you minute that, David?"

He looked up, annoyed at the break in his train of thought and also annoyed that he'd obviously missed something. Elias smiled genially and repeated the missed comment for his benefit. That there were no minutes for this meeting, and this was 'humour,' only registered a few seconds too late.

"...when they suggest you adopt crash positions on an aeroplane... it doesn't increase your chances of survival at all... it is only because that position helps them to identify your body from dental records if you die. It protects the mouth and teeth, you see..."

"I'm never flying again!"

David groaned inwardly, pushing the current soapy images fully to the back of his mind. The discussion was well off track now. The new programme wasn't that important, but he was damned if it would fail just because some people couldn't hold their attention on proper matters at appropriate times. He started to plan the best way to pull at the strings again from scratch.

Chp 14 – It Grows

The following weeks were very strange for David. In an impossibly short space of time, the reputation of and attention paid to the MITB website had sky-rocketed. Two months almost to the day from his first upload, David was sat in his office, ignoring phone calls and surfing Google (as he now did most days, at the expense of his university work). He very quickly found several new copycat sites, offering philosophical insights and sometimes sensible, (sometimes ridiculous) observations from a number of bizarre locations. They were springing up countrywide. He couldn't resist smiling at the conceit for a few of them. 'Man in a straitjacket' was one of his favourites so far, opening with a comment that the site would be very slow to be updated, as the straightjacket restricted movement, and every character had to be typed 'by nose'; 'Man in the shower' was a very poor 'vanilla' copy with understandably poor audio; 'Man in a motorcycle sidecar' also had serious sound issues; 'Man on the toilet' was amusing but disturbing. David's ultimate favourite was no doubt 'Girl in the Bath,' showing just how quick the adult entertainment industry picked up on new opportunities, though it wasn't exactly pearls of wisdom that the girl was showing. The fact that she reminded him of the exchange student didn't harm matters either.

He still studiously avoided looking at his own site from the work computer, a little paranoia creeping in, based around not wanting to leave any trail that might lead to identification, and knowing if he visited, he'd also feel compelled to log in and start replying to people. This was never quick, and extended logins to external sites might be tracked by HR or the I.T. department. Staying anonymous was a growing concern these days, what with the Community becoming so widespread and populous.

Three quarters of the morning had been taken up with meetings about finance and cohort development (a strange term the University had adopted that didn't really mean anything), but David couldn't concentrate on these any more. His mind was permanently elsewhere. Troubled, and elsewhere. Keeping his identity hidden hadn't been too difficult at first, and thankfully he didn't have any sort of strong regional accent, or use too many specific idioms that might narrow down a search for his real world details, but the attention was growing to critical levels, and it could only be a matter of time until somebody finally traced and tracked him down in the flesh world. David didn't want that. It was too much fun being the anonymous figure behind local and national speculation. There was now even footage on YouTube of an American chat show host referring to him and showing a clip of the 'Man in the Bath' on network television in the USA. The oddest, though gratifying, part was that the host had been booed when he'd made fun of it.

The videos themselves were growing less enjoyable to record, however. Now they tended to be less 'spur of the moment,' and were frequently on topics suggested by the Community. His initial intention not to comment on things that were already being discussed had quickly wavered, as he'd been bombarded with very polite but repeated questions, and the easiest way to answer them was to make a short clip. It was choice between doing that, committing to respond to individuals on a daily basis, or risk losing members by seeming deliberately rude or obtuse. David was also annoyed to admit that he was starting to feel genuinely obligated to his audience. The number of 'serious' questions directed his way had meant that the number of 'serious' replies had also increased. There were fewer and fewer musings on Shakespeare's accent, or the accuracy of The Da

Vinci Code, and more on real-world sociology, politics, and theology. David genuinely did seem to have helped some people with personal replies to queries, which was a great feeling, but it meant he had to treat the website quite a bit more sincerely than he'd first intended, even in his e-mails. That was less fun. Swings and roundabouts.

There were also now a number of sites springing up purely to commentate and update others on what the 'Man in the Bath' was saying, what he 'really meant,' and to debate his words. For some reason, rather than doing this on the actual Man on the Bath website itself, interested parties would comment from their own, narrower perspectives on their own social media platforms and blogs. Jumping the bandwagon, you might say. So, there was now an American 'Christians on Man in the Bath,' and a Middle Eastern 'Muslims on Man in the Bath.' Those were just examples from religious groups. Christ, there was now even the 'Man in the (Fathers for Justice) Bath' blogsite. It was hard for David to accept, but his creation was gathering attention like an avalanche. Of its own volition. The more people who wrote about it, the more direct attention and popularity it seemed to garner, regardless of whether the commentaries were supportive or negative. David blanked out as much of that sort of thing as he could, in an attempt to stay relatively sane and grounded. It was the best way to get your head round the phenomenon. If he thought too much about just how many people were paying attention to his own thoughts, then he'd be too terrified to ever speak again. By placing the recognition and popularity of the website in the category of 'interesting fact,' rather than thinking about how it related to him personally, he could partition cause from effect, and enjoy the experience. That was the internal reasoning he used.

The sexual offers had increased too, but had quickly ceased to be either entertaining or tempting, as David realised that the vast majority just wanted to know who he was, were borderline insane (most on the wrong side of the border line), or wanted their own fame as the woman (or man) who'd slept with him. Either that, or they were expecting something profound from a fuck. And he knew from personal feedback that he wasn't that good.

More disconcertingly, the 'Man in the Bath' (or 'Mint B' as some newspaper columnist had strangely and successfully nicknamed him), even crept into the Friday night pub discussions. David stayed very quiet when that happened, and found himself quite ironically almost totally excluded from some of the conversations, because of his lack of enthusiasm and views.

The first time that Tom had raised the topic of his alter-ego, it had been quite enjoyable, particularly when the guilty admissions started coming from his illustrious colleagues, that they all had a devotion to watching 'Mint B' videos as a secret vice. But that had rapidly started to go awry. One of the lecturers had started espousing and backing up the supposed 'views' of 'Mint B,' and the others had joined in. The problem was, they'd got the complete wrong end of the stick about the enlightenment bit he'd written. David couldn't help himself and had jumped in to correct them that first time, pointing out that it was obviously a bit of a wind up anyway, but that they'd missed the underlying principle that there was no solution. The vitriol that had come back had been quite shocking. He was shouted down from every side, Tyler Guthrie seemingly taking the correction personally and launching a retaliatory attack back at David, suggesting that he obviously didn't take it seriously himself, so shouldn't even <u>try</u> to contribute to the conversation, which should apparently be the preserve of the 'believers.' David had almost giggled at that terminology, despite everything else going on. Fortunately, Nadine hadn't been there as David had received continued abuse, and he'd ended up blushing in embarrassment as he was poked physically in the chest and accused of taking a 'Cliff's Notes,' or Wikipedia (blasphemy in academia) approach to the 'The Man in the Bath,' of knowing the words but not understanding the context or deeper meaning. A philosophy lecturer informed David that he didn't comprehend the very clever analysis and summarising of complex theories. Which almost prompted a retort that, they couldn't be that complex, if all it took was a smartarse and half a bottle of whisky to accidentally stumble on them.

The repeated implication that followed was that, as David wasn't a real academic, he couldn't be expected to understand. A part of him had still wanted to laugh, particularly when Tom had let slip that he was a member and one of the now almost infamous 'Community' himself. He'd explained proudly how they followed the 'teachings' of the Man in the Bath. Instead of the ridicule that would normally be expected for something like this, the admission was met with something almost approaching awe. David *really* wanted to reveal the truth right then, but the solidarity of the assembled staff made it feel oppressively like a school playground, and he was the kid who didn't fit in, and wasn't wanted. He'd stayed quiet instead, and sloped off soon after, unnoticed, frustrated at the inexplicable turn of events during the evening.

It was exhausting. David was frequently late for work now, and was well behind on his duties, even when he was present physically. It had been commented on. And this afternoon, the Head of the Department, Professor Cornwell, had asked to see him. Thankfully, in the evening he was due to go for a platonic meal with Nadine. Nadine had been the rock around which he'd tethered himself, and he'd even been tempted to confess the truth about his alter-ego to her once or twice but had bottled out.

#

"...so I think you need some rest David... I'm insisting you take some of the leave that's owed."

Professor Cornwell stared down his nose, through his round silver-rimmed glasses. David nodded, feeling like a student again.

"You need to have a proper break, and I don't want you working from home either. I'm not joking, David. Now, I don't like to criticise, but I know you think you can do everything, and you can't. To be blunt, your work is suffering. Which means the department is suffering. You're not concentrating."

It was hard to argue against the observation, but David still bristled under the words. He knew for a fact that Cornwell would never dare speak to his teaching staff like this. Like his predecessor, Professor Eric Blair, the Head of Department treated his academic colleagues with almost reverential respect in matters of their professionalism.

"I need to catch up on some things round the house anyway, and you're probably right, I have been tired lately. A couple of weeks then."

Professor Cornwell nodded sagely.

"I think that's very wise. Take longer if you need it."

His glasses slipped half an inch down his nose, turning the condescension into a comic spectacle. David nodded back, forcing a bland smile. Part of the anger was that he knew the observations were quite true, and that his work <u>had</u> been suffering. Most of the anger was for the fact it was being publicly pointed out.

"Why don't you get away for a few days? Paris is lovely this time of year!"

"I'd better go and organise things so there aren't any loose ends."

The trip down the stairs to his own office allowed David to calm himself through a controlled breathing exercise he knew, and to objectify what was happening. This wasn't actually a bad thing, if you did consider it dispassionately. Whilst the Professor obviously thought swanning round Paris with a guidebook would re-charge his batteries, the time off would mean he could seriously address the website and his online persona, without having to spend time thinking about his days in the 'flesh-world' job. Yes, this could actually work out quite nicely.

#

There was more of a spring in Dave's step as he headed to the bar to meet Nadine. It was like a weight had been lifted. His mind was still fully occupied though, this time with the question of whether he should fully admit to Nadine what the real problems were, and who his alter-ego was. Talk about how badly everybody was treating him, and his inability to justify himself without revealing that secret identity. He wondering if she'd sleep with him if he asked nicely and played the pity card. Dave shook that suggestion away as he pushed open the oak-panelled door and scanned the room for the familiar face, and chest.

She wasn't anywhere in sight, so he ordered a bottle of Cabernet Sauvignon, one he knew that she liked, and sat in the cleanest of the booths to wait. Everything had been getting admittedly close to being out of control recently, but today was unexpectedly improving. Two weeks off, time to reflect and take back proper control of the site. And a nice cosy drinks for two with the lovely Nadine. Yes, things were definitely looking up.

She arrived about ten minutes later, though David was a little disappointed to see non-flattering jeans, and a non-figure hugging, flirtation- free, sweater. She smiled as she sat down though, taking the proffered glass with a thank you.

"So… I hear you're on gardening leave?"

That rankled a bit. The term usually applied to forced absence for negative or job-threatening reasons. He forced a smile back.

"Not quite… Cornwell was right though. I have been overdoing it a bit recently. Didn't realise it was two years since I had a proper holiday… and what better way to start than sharing a glass of wine with an attractive colleague…"

He raised his glass. Nadine clinked hers against it in the requisite toast, but the half-smile she gave looked insincere. Dave hesitated, and began to re-think the 'coming clean' idea. It looked like she wasn't in a very sharing mood. They both sipped silently, listening to the strains of an old Northern Soul track leaking from the jukebox.

"So, what have you been up to?"

He asked to break the silence as much as anything, an empty feeling in his stomach that the nice evening and possibility of seduction was definitely off the cards. For tonight at least.

"Not much... marking... reading... checking out Mint B... I hear you had a conversation about him with some of the others?"

David's heart sank further. She couldn't have joined the acolytes as well. She was too feminist. And too intelligent.

"Kind of... we had a disagreement on... interpretation... Tom seems to think he has all these great insights... and no-one else is apparently allowed have an opinion..."

The words were carefully measured to be balanced, and not too detrimental, just in case. Nadine's frame seemed to relax slightly, and he felt relieved as he recognised the tell-tale indication of tension leaving her body. He hadn't even realised quite how stiff she'd been sitting. A warmer grin spread out across her full lips.

"I know what you mean... I had a bit of a disagreement with him too... over religion... Tom seems to think that Minty..."

The shadow of a frown.

"It's not too disrespectful calling him Minty, is it?"

Dave shook his head, stifling the urge to giggle, and studying Nadine's face. She smiled a broader smile.

"...that Minty should be followed like the Bible... taken literally in everything he says... to me its obvious that he... I mean he's said it openly... he's a guide rather than a literal leader, puts you on the path, points you in the general direction but isn't going to spoon feed you...."

"Exactly!"

Dave lifted his glass, cheered by the relief that Nadine, at least, wasn't being taken in completely by the apparent body snatcher phenomenon he'd sparked. Though she was obviously hooked for some reason. A wicked weasel of a plan flashed in front of his eyes. Involving Nadine e-mailing his alter-ego, and getting more than she bargained for in the way of lessons and penetrating epiphanies

"Then we got into religion per se... and Tom argues that it's a specifically Christian message, despite the enlightenment lesson..."

A furrow appeared in David's brow at the word 'lesson.'

"... whereas Minty is obviously allowing people to keep their own faiths, but gently steering them beyond the restrictions of a Church, guiding them to a point where they don't need formalised religious structures any more, but allowing them the crutch until they get there themselves."

David's shoulder's physically knotted, and he gritted his teeth to stop from pointing out it was just something he'd written quickly, while pissed, to stop people hassling him about another drunken lie, that such a guide existed at all. He wanted to point out he'd read the thing back recently and it made little, if any sense, just bits he'd picked up from a documentary on TV and thrown together. And that he was now starting to wish that he'd never started the whole bloody Man in the Bath identity in the first place. Hiding his mouth behind a sip of wine, he tried to keep his expression open and friendly, recognising the start of Steve Harley tune now playing in the background. The slow drink allowed him to try and look pensive and frame a suitable question.

"So... let me ask you Nade... the other... *insights*... aside... with his rather... powerful views on women... I'm quite surprised that you're being as... positive... as you are?"

Every word was chosen with great deliberation and care. It worked as planned, and her mahogany brown eyes seemed to sparkle with amusement.

"... what's your opinion on him as a whole...? I mean... <u>some</u> people seem to interpret him as quite misogynistic?"

It was bizarre to refer to yourself in the third person. Nadine just shrugged.

"... I think that's just one of those things... his approach... the way to get the message across... if you really study what he actually says, I think... I know he's very enlightened about feminism... to coin a phrase."

This was followed with an inviting grin.

"... and about women... If you ever met him Dave, I think you'd find that he was about as misogynistic as I am myself... if I didn't already know better, I'd think it was a woman writing... he certainly knows women... and what do I think of him...?"

She sucked her bottom lip between her perfect teeth in a very sexually alluring way, drawing air in. Dave found himself leaning fractionally closer.

"... let's just say that if Minty ever came across my path... I'd invite him in for coffee..."

Her eyes twinkled and she winked, the old flirtation back. Dave was torn. In another universe this admission would have had him whooping for joy, and vicariously admitting everything. As it was, the ill-advised words came out of his mouth before he'd finished thinking them.

"Have you ever e-mailed to tell him he could fuck you if he wanted to?"

She looked genuinely appalled.

"Dave! Don't be such a fucking pervert! Why would I do something like that?"

Nadine rarely swore in anger, and he mentally took a step back.

"Minty would be appalled too. You really haven't got a clue about him, have you?"

He bit back a sarcastic 'apparently not,' before it could escape his lips.

"He'd never do something like that. Never even think about it. It's well known that he's turned down a number of offers of sex point blank. The last woman in the Community got flamed till she left for suggesting that he'd taken her up on a sexual offer. We all know he's not like that."

Her anger settled a bit, fading as quickly as it had appeared.

"...I'd go to him if he wanted me, obviously... but I was talking about getting to know him, learning from him, not just sex. That would be incredible, obviously, but it would just be the icing on the cake."

Nadine had a faraway look in her eyes.

"No... he understands women, that's what I love about him... look at the pornography lesson..."

There it was again, lesson. And this from a feminist lecturer, an apparently intelligent one, who was swallowing his deliberately provocative ranting, as though it made sense. David had watched the whole raw footage on pornography back recently, after realising it had the most positive reviews, and had been amazed quite how much shit he'd been talking, and how the viewers couldn't seem to see the gaping holes in the logic.

"... he wants to empower women to accept their sexuality but only as a part of themselves... argues encouragement to embrace the sexuality of all women, and not be afraid of traditionally masculine outlets."

David's fists clenched under the table. No he doesn't, he just wants women to like porn as much as he does, and to make more of it. Nadine was on a roll though, and the more she spoke, the more he realised how smitten she was. And how misguided. If this was the reaction he was provoking in people, maybe he'd better start being a bit more explicit about what he actually meant. In the videos that weren't a wind-up anyway. David drained the glass and poured another one, right up to the rim. Maybe he should go back and review exactly how he'd managed to edit that porn rant into something so seemingly convincing. Whatever magic he'd applied in the editing suite, he seemed to have constructed a monster from the raw materials. One that was attracting women like flies round shit. It was too late to do anything about that one now, it was out in the world, and was too well known. He'd definitely go back to the original source video files again and see how he'd managed to cut it together so effectively. If he could discover what he'd done to make his words so convincing and influential, maybe he could use that method again, on something more important.

Chp 15 – Raising the Stakes

"Hi, Man in the Bath here again..."

The figure nodded his head in greeting. If you could see behind the blurred face, you would have seen the wine and whisky in his eyes. The voice had a little more to identify it today, but only if you knew the cracked and slightly raw tones of David under the influence of several hours' sustained drinking.

"Well, my children... today I'm afraid I'm going to be a bit controversial... not deliberately, but I know there's been some discussion of the 'big issues' in the Community, so let's start with one of the smallest of the big issues. As you know, I have no problems with anyone having their own beliefs or faiths... and I wouldn't mock them or demean them deliberately... but let me get one thing straight from the outset."

David steepled his fingers in the way he'd developed over the series of videos as his trademark, and then cracked his knuckles in the way he'd perfected as a mannerism, to flag he was about to deliver an important point. He reminded himself to try and keep sarcasm out of his voice as much as possible for this particular speech. It was important.

"If you're going to have intractable beliefs, it is always very, very advisable to..."

He paused again for dramatic effect in the normal way.

"... have a clue what the fuck you're talking about..."

This deserved and received another pause, and a small smile behind the pixilation. It deserved applause in fact. That had sounded really good, he thought.

"What I've been pondering for the last few days, is my position specifically on The Bible... with particular regard to those 'Church of England' Christians who take it literally. Now, I don't want to get off track here, so let's assume from the outset I'll ignore any hypocrisies of the religion itself, I won't even mention the absolutely wonderful conviction that it is near heresy for our next monarch to take the throne if they were divorced or getting married to a divorcee, I'll just suggest that some of those particular dissenters should read 'Henry the Eighth for Dummies.' No, today I want to talk about the book, the Holy book...."

David bit his lip, wanting to give full reign to all of his opinions, and be very explicit in his meaning, but with a little voice warning him it would be wise to hold back a little. Hopefully, some of the viewers, the more intelligent of them anyway, would already have made the link between the dangers of believing texts and believing websites.

"Now, elements of the Torah, the whole of the Koran, whatever your own faith... these books are the literal word of God, the Prophet, or of the prophets. No problem with that. But the New Testament... here's a vital question that seems to have eluded some of the most vociferous of our home-grown fundamentalist preachers, and that is... who actually wrote the fucking thing?"

David sank lower into the suds to allow the question to hang for a moment. And to hide a small belch of alcohol.

"... no-one with any scholarly interest whatsoever, and I include here all of the finest minds of the Christian Churches through the ages, thinks that God wrote it... oh no they don't, go and research the facts a little before you argue with me!"

That deserved yet another grin. The little grins and smiles were part of the routine now. He'd toyed with the interactive style of delivery before, but had always dismissed it as a bit pantomime.

Today he felt like pantomime was needed, so he didn't sound too much like a teacher.

"… and yet so many of them apply it as 'the Word of God,' inviolate, and with no room for manoeuvre or interpretation. All I'd like to humbly do at this point, is question this… not their faith, not their beliefs… just their Bible… let's look at the basic stages…"

David had rehearsed this part as he'd got gradually more drunk, since coming back from the bar after Nadine had left, a few hours earlier. That conversation hadn't gone the way he'd hoped it would, not even slightly. But the repetition of rehearsing this delivery, and the welcome 'other subject to focus on,' had occupied him in the way he'd needed as he got progressively more hammered. He wasn't <u>so</u> drunk that he slurred, and that was currently his only touchpoint for if he should stop, but David was certainly drunk enough for his speech to come freely. And freely it had come, as he worked out what he wanted to say and how it might double as a repudiation of those taking him too seriously. Rehearsing the actual words he was going to deliver from the bath was a new practice, and went slightly against the original premise of spontaneity, but with the importance people were placing on his words, he wanted to make sure that he didn't make any mistakes this time. He hadn't accounted for the fact that sustained drinking can leave you able to talk and feel like you're sober, when the reality is quite different, and your judgement is less than perfect.

"... let's narrow it down even more and take the gospels... and let's assume for now that there actually *was* a Jesus, and his message *was* roughly what we all believe now, and nothing to do with cheesemakers... though that is actually quite a good example... whatever he said or didn't say on the Mount, and he could have liked cheese for all we know... the words went from mouth to mouth in an extreme version of Chinese Whispers for fifty to two hundred years before they were written down, that we know of... and this isn't like the Koran, when the exact words were repeated and learned by rote... it was a time of political upheaval... educated and uneducated Christians passing on the message, rather than the exact speech... but for now, let's gullibly believe that somehow the exact words were all remembered, in the right order. They then got written down... probably in Aramaic... which uses a fantastic alphabet without any vowels... I saw a wonderful program on TV once, that pointed out, without the benefit of context or modern interpretation, that one particular section could be read either as

'Jesus forgave them' or 'Jesus fucked them' – in the sense of executed them, that is..."

David licked his dry lips. Talking did that. There was a whole section he'd missed out there. He's got side-tracked again. He was supposed to have mentioned the inconsistencies in the gospels. He decided on the hoof not to go back. The words were flowing now, and he didn't want to stop them. It was starting to feel vaguely good, and he didn't want to lose that feeling. This was starting to feel a bit more like the old rants.

"... so, we have a load of scrolls and codices with the gospels on... quite a number actually... and someone, somewhere, decided which ones would be official canon... well a number of people did actually, but, believe it or not, this was *still* a difficult time for Christianity, politically speaking, what with the lions and all that, and we've had spin doctors for far longer than the average layman imagines. I know we think that modern politics only invented them a few decades back, but a bloke called Machiavelli had a few similar ideas 500 years ago, and he learned his trade from the Greeks and Romans, but I digress... again... "

David frowned, finding it hard to stick to the point, and even harder to remember the script now. Sometimes free-flowing remarks weren't such a good idea, but he desperately didn't want to lose the good feeling of just letting his words come of their own accord, so he soldiered on. 'You can edit later,' he told himself. ɪDon't worry, you can edit later.'

"... so, already we've got Chinese whisper words, written in an open-to-interpretation alphabet, and the most politically unacceptable or inconvenient scrolls being quietly forgotten, ones purportedly by minor characters like Mary, mother of the Christ...! Anyway, this then gets translated into Greek, and into Latin from the Greek, and we all know how accurate translations can be, depending on the translator... but let's for now assume that the words and stories miraculously survived all this passing on and translation. Then we get to the British, and good old King James... now, the cynics amongst you might question Jimmy's motives for having his name on the official Bible, Divine Right, and all that, but aside from the ego trip, good old King Jim wasn't being quite as altruistic as you might think when he gave Britain the Bible in the English language."

David knew he was wandering all over the place now, that colloquialisms were creeping in more than usual, and this hadn't been the intended track of the speech at all, but he just couldn't stop himself. There was no choice but to drop the intended script completely, and just see where the words took him.

"... there were already lots of Bibles in English, you see... and that was the problem... putting the holy message and words directly into the reach of the common man meant that the interpretation of what it meant to be Christian was no longer the preserve of the priests... when it was in Latin and no-one understood the words for themselves, people would do as they were told... the big danger was that a direct line to the Scripture meant people might not need the Church any more, and it was getting too late to put that cat back in the bag. So the Church, in its infinite wisdom, executed anyone creating or reading a Bible in English, calling it blasphemy... look it up if you don't believe me... look it up if you do actually, it's fascinating, and it's always good to read... All the Church histories mention it, even if they don't dwell on it. So anyway, King Jimmy was in a bit of a fix, and his spin doctors had a classy idea. Produce an official version of the Bible in English. Now here's the clever bit. Jimmy's monks put their heads together and drafted a few Bibles, as you do, then someone had a bright idea of how to persuade people that this was the best version... forge it!"

David did pause for breath at this point, feeling nicely controversial, and remembering the one word he'd intended to use all along. Getting the word 'forge,' was second best only to using the word 'fake' in his speeches. He wanted to put them in every single one, so someone paying close attention could rumble him. One of the many hundreds of people now deconstructing his words and website at the water cooler.

"They wrote a version using as many archaic words and phrases as they could think of, so if you compared the text to one of these new-fangled printed Bibles, it would sound more venerable and older, and as we all know, if it's older then it must be truer. I really do urge you to go and look all this up for yourselves by the way, don't take my word for it, its well documented, quite amusingly by the Church itself... so anyway, Jimmy's official Bible™ could tinker with the translations a bit more, to make them fit the Church and State policies of the day, and it would appear to be more genuine than the other versions, which were, of course, fake in the eyes of the clergy."

There it was. Fake. Both words included. He nodded to himself in congratulation.

"... then King Jim could mandate his version, claim the credit, and let everyone know what a remarkable thing he'd done, by bringing the Scripture to the common man."

David rose out of the water (well, lifted his chest out anyway), to deliver the summation of his sermon.

"So... the next time the village busybody quotes the Bible at you as God's law, feel free to ask them who wrote the fucking thing in the first place. Personally, I think Jesus might be a little bit pissed off if he was alive today. Here endeth the lesson... next time I might point you in the direction of Christmas and the birth of Jesus, and make you look up what Yule originally meant, before you tuck into your swiss roll Yule Log, and then ask you to look up the strange co-incidences with the life and mythology of Mithras and find out, if you can, the first time anyone actually bothered to mentioned virgin mothers, stables, donkeys and gifts in relation to Jesus Christ. I'm guessing virgin mothers and being reborn in caves was quite a common occurrence in those days, as it didn't get much of a mention in Christianity for a couple of hundred years. And as I don't want Christians to feel too picked on, I might point out where the Mithras origin story was nicked from too. This is the Man in the Bath, signing off."

It was a rambling mess going everywhere with half-formed thoughts at the end, but damn, it had felt good to say. He beamed at the video camera, knowing anything said at this point would be cut out at the editing stage.

"Excellent job, David."

He tilted his head and ran his fingers through his wet, slicked back hair.

"Why, thank you David."

"That should ruffle a few feathers, David."

"You think so, David?"

"I do, David. That's why you did it. And hopefully some of the poor sods out there won't feel too embarrassed when they realise you're full of shit."

"Let's hope so, David."

With the conversation finished, he sank lower into the rapidly cooling water.

"How do you reconcile wanting this to go away with doing more clips?"

He submerged his head and held his breath for twenty seconds, coming up panting. Not answering his own question. It was self evident. It was fun. He answered a different question instead.

"Another drink, David? Why yes, I don't mind if I do, to celebrate, to us!"

Chp 16 – Backlash

David Dunn's head was ringing as he peeled his eyes open and stared at the bright red neon of his alarm clock, showing ten am. He'd stayed up very late, and had got very drunk. Again.

He staggered towards the bathroom and splashed copious amounts of icy water onto his face and hair, gasping at the shock of the wetness on his hungover and hot skin. Then he scowled into the mirror and headed into the kitchen to put on the kettle and make a large mug of very milky instant coffee.

Leaning on the countertop, with the noise of the kettle just starting to rise, his recent memories swam back to the surface. Not entirely sure of the sequence of events, he did know for certain that he'd ended up baiting a number of religious groups the previous last night, with an alcohol-induced lack of tact. And he wasn't entirely sure that all, if any, of the facts he'd quoted had been correct. That hadn't been the only argument last night, or even the first.

It hadn't been the video on the Church at the root of the conversation last night, that had been posted several days ago. No, this time he'd entered into actual debate on his own forums under an assumed name, rather than as the Administrator, and had claimed to personally know and understand the true meanings of the 'Man in the Bath' videos. He couldn't remember why he'd used an assumed name, or how he'd claimed authority for knowing, but it had seemed quite reasonable at the time.

Though several people had questioned the validity of his identity as an 'insider,' a large enough section of the Community had initially believed, or had been open to his thoughts that David had been able to develop and espouse his genuine views at length. He'd been quite open and forthright that the 'Man in the Bath' was trying to provoke a reaction, rather than claiming to provide any sort of genuine, insightful, wisdom.

David settled into the comfortable green armchair and pulled a blanket over his knees, cupping his mug, and sipping at the burning but enlivening liquid within. It had been the responses of other people that had started it all.

One of the video clips from a couple of weeks ago had facetiously suggested that the problem of welfare benefit costs could be solved by simply stopping people from having the automatic right to children. That Man in the Bath video had suggested the problem was caused by irresponsible parents, not those who wanted and loved their numerous children. In a flippant aside, he'd suggested that people be employed in State-run orphanages, that all automatic rights to child benefit be suspended, and that those that those who couldn't afford their family would hand over their children to the orphanage.

On eloquent and unfiltered form, and pushing his argument to it's natural conclusion, David, or rather, the 'Man in the Bath', then suggested that these parents should be made to work in the orphanage themselves, in order to pay for their own children's upkeep, and those that refused initially should have all their other benefits rescinded, and should be forced to work and pay support to the childcare institutions, on pain of jail. Real jail. No-one had picked up on the fact that David was effectively suggesting the return of the Victorian workhouse, with a slight twist.

He could almost feel a physical twinkle in his eye as he remembered inventing that argument. He'd immensely enjoyed putting together a cogent internal logic, and had recorded it primarily as a joke, posting on the first of April, April Fool's Day, deliberately. The smile faded. Last night he'd first noticed a new thread from some members of the Community, who he'd previously ignored as being deluded but harmless, but who were seriously and actively debating the proposal; arguing how it could work in practice, and suggesting a petition be put together for Parliament for the creation of the 'benefit work orphanage.' That was when David's drinking had properly started. Partly to occupy his hands while he decided whether to ban the thread, delete it, or join the debate and point out he hadn't been serious. It had taken longer to decide than he'd anticipated.

David knew from experience that if you pushed the bubble down in one place, it would just pop up somewhere else and he'd spent almost an hour talking himself through the probable outcomes of each potential response to these idiots, growing angrier and drinking more and more as he did so. If you couldn't even be flippant, then a lot of the enjoyment and satisfaction was taken from the whole MITB enterprise. On the flip side, a dark shadow on his other shoulder reminded David that he enjoyed the attention he received immensely, and that he had a 'sort of' responsibility for any subsequent reactions himself. The pride was still there that he'd created the Community in the first place. And they did look up to him. He knew specific examples, quite a number now, where it seemed that he had actually made a tangible difference to some real people's lives, with the things that he'd said in personal replies. Not an enormous difference, he was still self-aware enough to realise that, but to some people, he'd shown a genuine compassion, and made a genuine difference. That was the reason for his 'informed insider' appearance on the boards, to try and set the record straight about an inconsequential and flippant video, so it was clear that this was different to his more serious and helpful side. To make sure the website stayed close to its original purpose and wasn't subverted by misunderstanding. It had all made perfect sense at the time, last night. David almost dropped his cup as he gulped a too-large gulp, and burned the roof of his mouth, panting open-mouthed.

"Let them work to pay the State for raising their own children. Let parents who are responsible do what they want, but no procreation without indemnification."

That had been the end of the video, and was the actual quotation that had started last night's debate. At first, his repudiation of the post as a wind-up had seemed to be working, arguing that it was a provocation rather than a genuine suggestion, with the sole purpose of getting people talking about the important and wide ranging issues around welfare benefits and their history.

He'd even explicitly pointed out the workhouse parallels and how awful they had been for the poor, and the quite telling fact that the video had been posted on April Fool's Day.

The first responses had been measured, interested, and had seemed as though the Community was accepting, or at least listening to and considering, the suggestion that this particular video talk was not intended to be taken seriously. Even though the username he'd been using had never appeared before, and there was no evidence given as to why this voice understood more than anyone else about the 'Man in the Bath,' he had been listened to with some respect. He'd started to think it was working, that his viewers would respond to reason if he only explained things more clearly.

The apparent respect continued until the conversation had switched onto other, wider topics. Alcohol had overcome caution, and David had started to explain the 'true' meaning of some of the religious-themed videos, and particularly, the recent 'Church' one, of a few nights previous. Things had quickly got heated. The deference had disappeared. Several members of the Community became abusive. And David was suddenly the object of scorn, and accused of being a 'troll,' deliberately trying to mislead 'the Community.' Then, the 'flaming' had begun in earnest.

Unable to get himself heard on his own website, David had searched for those other messageboards which he knew existed, who debated the 'Man in the Bath' posts, the several faith-based ones, hoping to find a better reaction there. He found every possible misinterpretation of what he'd said being put forth, and had waded into a number of these debates recklessly, several windows open on his computer at once, as he 'corrected' CoE, Jewish, Catholic, any commentator he could find who had a faith-based view, on how they'd misunderstood the videos and messages. The corrections had not been tactful, and had mainly consisted of pointing out that all religious institutions were deeply flawed. It was only at the realisation he was typing the wrong replies in the wrong windows, and had been for some time, and that his last reply had accused one Jewish poster of being a bad Catholic, that he'd admitted to himself that it was probably time to stop.

#

One important personal relationship had changed slightly since the break-up with Liz.

Although Nadine had been fine with him for the first day or so, Dave had now taken to phoning her up whenever he needed somebody to talk to, something he'd never done previously. While outwardly fine with the calls, there was now an underlying nervousness on Nadine's part when they met, as though only her innate politeness made his former partner-in-crime refrain from telling him to stop altogether. The relationship hadn't been helped by their 'Man in the Bath' conversation.

Dave had tried to refrain, but with everything that had happened the night before, he'd felt the irresistible urge to talk to someone, even though he didn't yet feel comfortable enough to confide all the details to her. Deep down, he'd known it would be a bad idea, but David Dunn had been short on options. Previous conversations in similar circumstances hadn't turned out well, but sitting alone at home and dwelling on the situation had been starting to drive him crazy.

So Dave had phoned Nadine and invited her for a drink. And now that they were here, he didn't really know what to say. He just needed the company.

"So... what's happening with you?"

Nadine shuffled on her chair a fraction and sipped at her drink, surreptitiously but very obviously checking her watch as she did so. There was no short skirt or low-cut top again tonight.

"Not a lot. I'm meeting a friend in a while though. I used to share a flat with her, and I haven't seen her for ages."

Dave was fairly sure this was a lie. He didn't really mind Nadine not wanting to be there, he just didn't like lies.

"Really? What's her name?"

There was a tell-tale pause.

"... Sam... Samantha..."

"And what's she up to?"

Nadine crossed her legs and hid her mouth with her drink, draining half of the remaining liquid. Her reply sounded testy.

"I don't know... like I said, I haven't seen her for ages."

"Oh. And where are you two going? A nice restaurant? The Playhouse?"

David didn't really want to know, but if he wasn't going to get the companionship he craved himself, then he'd at least make it difficult for her to leave. Nadine's patience had already run out though.

"A bar... I don't know. Look... what is it you wanted Dave?"

His mouth opened and then closed again wordlessly, as he realised that he didn't have an answer to that. He shrugged instead, mumbling something vague and bland about wanting company. Nadine softened slightly (but only slightly), as she emptied her glass completely.

"I'm not your girlfriend, Dave. We work together. That's all!"

There was a finality to ither words Then a pitying half-smile, and she got up and left.

Chp 17 – Higher Echelons

David locked the door of the office and pulled a quarter bottle of scotch out of his desk drawer, pouring a generous measure, and swigging it down in one. Rumours were rife, and there was a pervasive excitement in the staffroom. The e-mail had been circulating round all the university staff, and he needed some liquid confidence before looking it up to read for himself. That was why he'd crept back into work so early, despite the enforced 'leave.'

Google news had it as the top story for the UK. At Prime Minister's question time, one of the MPs had asked about the 'Community,' the huge and almost formal organisation who followed the wisdom of the 'Man in the Bath.' Sections of the 'Community' had apparently been lobbying for a new bill: 'No Procreation Without Indemnification.' And someone in the House had asked for the Prime Minister's view. The surprising thing, and the thing that had made it newsworthy, was that the answer had been hedged. The proposed bill had thankfully been rejected of course, but the Prime Minister had referred to the will of the people, and that 'The Man in the Bath' was providing a service by promoting widespread discussion of political issues. The fact he was enthusing people to participate in the democracy was a fantastic thing, though the Prime Minister wouldn't be drawn on individual topics. A follow up question had elicited an admission that he'd visited the site several times, and what he found there had been interesting, entertaining, and valuable. And that Stuart Sutcliffe was his choice as the fifth Beatle. That had got a laugh.

Cross-party, there had been voices praising the idea of a platform for common people who had no voice in traditional party structures, and while everyone was angling to take credit for a number of ideas, the political commentators suggested that the size and volume of subscribers to the site had the politicians worried.

The e-mail contained details of the news story, but also contained a petition to be sent to the Vice-Chancellor of the University on behalf of the Student Union, asking that the institution officially support the revised bill when it was re-submitted.

Finished with reading, David swigged down the rest of the bottle and then coughed violently. He ignored the knock on the door and sat down in his chair, swinging round to face the window. He wasn't officially in work, was he? He was on leave. And his hobby was starting to get seriously out of hand.

#

That evening, a new voice joined the Community on the website. This one didn't enter into debate or details, but in a single, sober post, attempted a rational deconstruction of the 'Man in the Bath.' It was deliberately non-confrontational. The reasonable voice politely pointed out that some posters in the Community were starting to take the clips far too seriously, and were clearly missing the point, though any debate was, of course, laudable. It went on to calmly remind everyone that the mysterious 'Man in the Bath' obviously didn't mean his own views to be taken literally, and that some of them were clearly meant to be jokes, or at least humorous, as indicated in the clips themselves. It was a single post, and he deliberately used different grammar and a softer tone than his previous attempt. It was anonymous and claimed no insight or direct connection to the MITB himself.

At nine pm David started drinking again, taken aback by the huge volume of 'flame' responses, abuse and insults this post had received. At ten pm, not even sure how it happened, he found that the new voice and account he'd just used had been banned from his own site, and that he couldn't log in under that name any more. A character naming himself 'The Priest' claimed credit, and warned that it was time to keep a tighter control on the content of posts, that anyone else showing disrespect to 'The Man in the Bath' would be likewise dealt with. This was met with what seemed to be universal approval in the Community. And for the first time Dr David Dunn was a little scared.

That was when he went for a walk, intending to clear his head and instead doing the opposite, as he visited the off-license to purchase more scotch.

Chp 18 – Balancing the Argument

"Hi, Man in the Bath here again… thought I'd share a little thought with you all… perhaps as a balance to one of my earlier pieces…"

David soaped his chest as he talked, relaxing into his subject, which this time had sprung from a genuine germ of revelation while waiting for the bus to Sainsbury's. A genuine germ, and a desire to try and reclaim the original vision for these videos, and to try and take the site back to its original roots.

After being kicked out of his own message forum, David's first instinct had been to pull the whole toyhouse down. But there were two problems with that. Firstly, how to do it in such a way that he wouldn't drown the baby with the bathwater, as he still clung to the hope that the original idea could be rescued. Second, and less easy to admit to, David was becoming very addicted to making the clips. As scary as the adulation could potentially be, it was extremely hard to give up a position where people wanted to hear what you had to say, and valued it. Perversely, the reactions out in the 'real world' also meant that talking in the bath was now the only place David felt truly relaxed, and able to express himself without worrying. Deep down, he was aware this was a potentially dangerous situation.

Talking to the camera in the bath was second nature now, comforting, and let him say what he really felt. Apart, ironically, from talking about the 'Man in the Bath' phenomenon. Even at his most drunk, he knew better than to enter into any debate or discussion about his 'sermons' within the videos themselves, and now rarely responded to e-mails, and never if they related to who he was, or what his opinion might be on something specific.

A perverse logic deep within David had therefore reasoned that the best way forward was to keep posting, but to try and make the opinions less accessible, or popular. This would hopefully kill off the parasitic Community from the roots, but allow him to keep making and posting distracting little videos for his own amusement. He had been especially looking forward to making this one. This was going to be his first explicitly and unable to be misconstrued, 'think for yourself' message, allowing himself space to gradually back out of the other debates, while hinting that this had been the ultimate intention all along.

"As you may have surmised from some of the things I've said earlier, I'm not a big one for formal, organised, religion, and have many doubts and questions over them. But I *am* quite a spiritual person, and my own personal views on a designated higher sentient power are best saved for another time rather than right here, right now. In short response to the number of posts on other sites quoting me as support for various atheist, agnostic or non-believing groups, let me ask you one simple question and you can work out the answer for yourselves..."

He dropped the soap and raised his arms to fold his hands behind the back of his neck, under his ponytail.

"How come apples are so fucking nice?"

David let the question hang and picked up the flannel, washing his chest and letting the video run on. This continued for almost three minutes before he couldn't resist speaking again. That length of silence could be edited later if necessary. David raised his head, as though just realising he was still being filmed. He was in a particularly good mood today for some unknown reason. Maybe it was that he was properly back at work and in a routine, that he'd had been sober for several days, that he felt vaguely healthy for the first time in weeks. Or maybe it was that he had a clear plan.

"What? You need more? You want me to spoonfeed it to you? Okay, just another couple of queries, and you can answer these questions yourselves. You're all grown up now... so, intelligent design in all of its variables has plenty of flaws, there's no doubt about that, but one grain of truth... no... I know... let me give you a real example instead, of my problem with many people who espouse religion AND its alternatives... They don't think it through for themselves. A guy I knew once, very intelligent guy... highly intelligent... we were talking about religion in a group, and I asked him the question how he knew God existed. He looked surprised I'd asked, and said "just look at the sky, the trees... they exist! Everything exists!" and to him, existence itself proved that his God existed and was responsible... now there's a sentence that would be difficult to pull off after a couple of vodkas. It brought to mind a wonderful tautological question... if existence itself proves God is there, because he created it, then there was presumably a time before God did his little creation thing. At which point, there was no existence. If there was no existence, at all, surely that means that God didn't exist. Unless God created himself. And how could He create anything before He himself had been created? Convoluted I know, and I'm not convinced myself... it sounded better in my head... but my point is... a better response from this guy, let's call him Barry, when asked how he knew if God existed, a better response from Barry would have been... "Why do apples taste so fucking nice?"

David smiled to himself. This was the little question that had first popped into his brain on the way to Sainsbury's, but had then genuinely occupied it for about three subsequent hours, prompting this spiel.

"... now, so far as I'm aware, none of the religious groups, the mainstream ones anyway, argue that fruit and vegetables are sentient, yet the apple has developed to be so tasty that we want to spread its seed... sorry...? ... what's that?"

He was enjoying himself tremendously tonight. This was the kind of wandering dissemination of insight that he'd wanted from the beginning. Stream of consciousness. Not the Virginia Woolf crap, real stream of consciousness thought.

"What's that? Evolution, survival of the fittest? Good question, but if you really think it through, the question supports the idea of an intelligent design or influence – which was actually what Darwin said if you read his works... he was very religious, as a matter of fact. Now, I understand the process of natural selection, mutation, all that, but it doesn't happen overnight. It happens over a huge amount of time, and it would be incredibly fortuitous if so many things had developed in such a short space of time, cosmologically speaking. The modern apple is a relatively new creation, ethno-botanically. You should read this fantastic book by a bloke called Wade Davis by the way, 'One River', it's fascinating. Nothing to do with apples, but in the ball park of some of these themes. But I digress... The apple is a remarkably simple example.... And before the God-botherers mention Adam and Eve, two more points... One, if homo sapiens existed in Eden, then it's still a fairly recent time in ethno-botanical terms. Secondly, although King James's Bible names an apple, the earliest original copies of the texts don't... they actually say it was a pear, or something, I forget. I personally suspect that King James just had a personal aversion to apples, an unpleasant experience maybe, so he didn't want anyone else to like them either... or the reverse, maybe he wanted to put everyone else off so he could keep all of the apples to himself..."

David gasped a breath as his lungs ran out of steam, unable to keep pace with the monologue pouring from his brain.

"... To better illustrate my point, let's look instead at the rather less controversial topic of the fig wasp... and there's a sentence you don't hear every day... now the fig wasp, or for that matter any number of species of bee and wasp.... A number of plants have somehow evolved to create flowers that look exactly like wasp pussy, and these wonderful flora are actually pollinated on a wasp's cock. Or something like that, anyway, I forget the exact details. Might have been their legs, but there has definite dry-humping involved. Go watch a David Attenborough clip if you want to find out its name. My point is, plants have evolved quite specifically to attract specific animals as pollinators. And the chances of that happening independently, and so specifically in the hundreds of thousands of ethno-botanical relationships between plants and animals is unbelievable. If plants aren't sentient, and natural selection develops as gradually as the scientists would have you believe, then some of these bizarre relationships can only support the argument for some greater force or intelligence. With a sense of humour."

David propped himself up onto his elbows, leading up to the end point he'd come up with that afternoon in the office, aware that he had been rambling even more than usual up to this point.

"If you don't believe me, then let's all get together and have a massive experiment. Everyone in the world should use an apple corer and, critically, burn the seeds before eating the apples. If I'm right, within a couple of generations apples will taste less appealing to man, as they aren't fulfilling their side of the pollination deal, and the unpleasant ones propagated by other means will flourish and become the dominant remaining species of apple instead. Of perhaps a strain will develop to start smelling of rotting flesh to attract flies instead. Thus proving God is dead... This is the Man in the Bath, the conduit of a higher intelligence, signing off..."

He nodded to himself smugly, self-satisfied. That should be ridiculous and incoherent enough to start killing off the popularity of the videos as wisdom. And there was still a kernel of an interesting debate in there at the same, if you looked closely enough, which pleased David greatly. He would resist the urge to edit too much before posting, except for the long silence. Leave some of the best inconsistencies in to be discovered. Don't force it, let them discover the flaws and think for themselves. But hopefully about apples too. He was proud of that analogy. Totally nonsensical but with a ring of philosophy.

David didn't even really like the taste of apples himself, and they gave him heartburn.

Chp 19 – The Administrator

The next week passed in a total blur. The first day officially back at work hadn't quite been so bad. Until he'd started overhearing whispered conversations everywhere. For the three days after that one, he'd phoned in sick, not wanting to have to try and concentrate on mundanities like his job, or hear himself discussed in the third person. Each of the three days ended in the bottom of a bottle. The good feelings had gone. The reaction to his 'wisdom' was swelling even further. The sheer volume of misinterpretation and press coverage was astounding.

David decided that he needed to do some in-depth research, to find out just how immense a monster he might have actually created. One of the very first discoveries was an example of what turned out to be a veritable host of 'associated' sites. These weren't copycats; they were apparent shrines to some of his more provocative ramblings. The first site he'd come across had contained a word for word transcription of his rant about the destruction of apple seeds. Only a few days old, it already had over 1000 names signed up to the appeal at the bottom, promising to perform the experiment, just as he had jokingly suggested. The site was hosted by a group called 'Atheists for the truth.' And this for the most transparently ridiculous post so far.

By the end of the third day, a now dishevelled and unwashed but seriously obsessed David Dunn came across a news item that left him cold. In the mid-West of America, a group called 'Christians against the Church' had staged a mass bible-burning, citing the 'Man in the Bath' as a supporter, and calling for the dissolution of the Christian Churches and their 'institutional lies.' Two people died in the riot which had followed.

Any enjoyment that there had ever been in writing the blog, or making the clips, had vanished along with that sobering news. And there was no-one to confide in, no-one to tell, no-one to turn to for advice. At first, he'd attempted to convince himself this was just a tragic co-incidence, and David had clung desperately to the assertion that the connected sites were nothing to do with him, or what he did; that he was just being used as a brand vehicle, to promote someone else's movement.

But he'd been compelled to check further on that particular news story and had been truly horrified by what he'd found. A whole section of the literature on the 'Christians against the Church' website quoted him, word for word, before summing up the 'twisting of Christianity,' and the 'perversion of the True Word,' in what they called 'The Corrupt Church's Satanic Bible.' They'd actually taken him at his word. Literally. They'd used his words; *'They wrote a version using as many archaic words and phrases as they could think of'*... *'tinker with the translations to make them fit the Church and State policies of the day,'* ' *here's a vital question...who wrote the thing?'* The swearing was gone, but the rest of his words were there, expanded with references for further reading. And these seemingly genuine, committed Christians had taken his word over that of their former Church. Normally he'd have been immensely proud of that, but now, he was just sickened.

Granted, there was an underlying motive which he'd discovered when delving a little deeper, and the true driving force seemed to be a fervent and obsessive American patriotism. It was clearly the King James Bible specifically that the group was targeting, and a small section mentioned that some of 'their own' scholars were creating a 'true, American Bible' for the faithful. But the fact remained. People had died. People had died, and his words had sparked, and been used to incite the riot that had caused human death.

This was why David couldn't keep his mind focused on anything else. This was why there was a creeping sensation of dread and helplessness, amplified by the copious amounts of alcohol. That was why this week was a nightmare. He daren't write or record anything more and was afraid to go outside in case someone magically identified him and brought him to justice for the things done in his name.

#

By the seventh day, David had forced himself back into a more rational frame of mind, but was still afraid to go on his own website, worried about what he might end up posting if he did, and the reaction it might get. He'd started considering every other event with a growing paranoia. He was worried that 'The Priest,' whoever they were, now seemed to have access to the administrative controls. So David had taken a step back, taken stock, and had stopped drinking again.

He phoned into the University and booked another week's holiday, complaining of stress and being met with a sympathetic ear by the Head of Department, who confided that he was glad David seemed to be finally taking his health seriously, and urged him to take even longer if it was needed.

That had felt a little patronising, but Dr David Dunn had smiled and nodded on the other end of the phone through gritted teeth, telling himself that the outcome was all that mattered. It was nine days already since his last update of the site, although he was now back to nervously checking the comments section several times a day, without ever posting a word.

The Community didn't seem to mind his absence, with several suggestions and suppositions that he was away being profound elsewhere, one even reporting that he'd heard it was an audience with the Dalai Llama. Another time this would have been amusing, but now it just heightened the sense of frustration and annoyance, at the insanity of the situation.

It was a strangely innocuous realisation, on the following Saturday afternoon, which had finally decided the next course of action for David. He'd been at the coffee house, reading a Saturday newspaper, and had been unsurprised that the 'Man in the Bath' was now featured in the pages several times. The report of the Alabama riot mentioned the reference to his video in some detail, but it didn't blame him in any way, and it was actually the creeping guilt he felt for this, for not being blamed in the article, which had forced him into formulating a new plan; to take concrete action, and make a serious attempt at restitution.

At eight am the next day, David sat down and started to type a long document to upload onto another fresh website. If he couldn't influence the Community, he could create a new one to replace it. If he could do it once, then he could do it again. And this new Community would put the record straight, put the real truth out there, or as much of it as his creeping paranoia would allow. He would create the Community and all their beliefs anew, but make it better, more carefully, more in his own true image.

The document to upload was called '*Man in the Bath – debunking the myth,*' and it detailed the genuine truth behind some of the previous postings. The new website he set up, a small, free one, was called Justmythoughts.com. David was careful not to give his real identity away, but carefully pointed out the specific inconsistencies in the original Man in the Bath videos and posts, mistakes, and contradictions he'd noticed later, the April fools' joke (and the date it was posted), the genuine reasons for him starting the entire enterprise in the first place. He then quickly logged into the original site and put a bright and prominent hyperlink on there, directing anyone with a rational part of their mind remaining to the new site, where they could find 'the real truth.' He pushed the new website and its sole, revelatory document, live at 11am, and then went out to the shops to stock up his fridge, a weight lifted that he'd done something definitive, positive, and constructive.

David logged back on to <u>Justmythoughts.com</u> first, at 4pm after unpacking the shopping, and his heart plummeted with the discovery that the new site had already been hacked, and the confessional explanation removed. Not just that, but even the homepage had been altered. When you tried logging onto the URL of the 'Justmythoughts' site now, a message that read 'Dissolved by The Priest' flashed up for twenty seconds, and then took his browser straight to a porn site which crashed the computer. The feelings of helplessness and paranoia returned tenfold.

Chp 20 – Sea Change

"All of it?"

"Yes, all of it. That's what I said!"

David snapped at the barber. Part of it was vexation at life in general, part of it was a genuine queasiness. He'd had long hair for twenty years, and while this drastic change was a statement, an outward sign of intent to change his life, an end-note to his alter-ego, there was a distinct nervousness about the act itself.

"Whatever you say, boss."

David closed his eyes and exhaled slowly, trying to calm his nerves. The Man in the Bath was finally over now, for good. Late in the previous evening he'd been back onto the original site and posted what would be his final message at the top of the comments section, locked at the very top of the page, and closing down all further opportunities to respond by freezing the site. It had been a very deliberate and methodical plan. And a deliberate retirement. He'd finally plucked up the courage, and was proud that he'd managed to remain sober enough to formulate and execute this final plan. To unequivocally put an end to the madness.

That had been yesterday, in preparation, and just three hours ago David had removed the Man in the Bath website totally, resisting the urge for even a final look at it while it was still (a)live. The pause from the night before had been to allow search engine bots to poll the page, and then hold that final version in their cache. He allowed himself a little kudos at that part of the plan, proud of his own ingenuity. It had been a dilemma that David had been puzzling over since he'd made the decision, how to retire the 'Man in the Bath' in a way that wouldn't allow any alteration to his final message from hackers. A bit of online research had taught him how to do it, and how to make sure the search engines did a sweep to pick up the latest, and last version of the site. Now, when people couldn't log onto the web address itself, he hoped they'd search with Google. A search would allow those dedicated enough to pick the 'cache' page; the last version recorded by the search engine. And that last version would show his retirement message at the top. Unable to be altered. A dignified end to the whole mess. And it would let David get his life back.

His momentary self-congratulation was disturbed by the sounds of the scissors snipping.

David's body tensed, and all thoughts of the website vanished as he felt his hair pulled tightly into a bunch at the back, and then felt the sharp blades start to hack through the thick knot of ponytail. He kept his eyes closed, not wanting to see the result, as he gulped down a sensation of nausea.

The intended change in image was to help him break all connection with his online alter-ego, and the self-recrimination he inspired, but there was a distinct regret now, that he hadn't researched the local hairdressers better. The focus of David Dunn's mind locked onto what he would look like at the end of this visit, and he started to imagine all of the possible hairstyles he could have, and how they might change people's perceptions and attitudes towards him. He ignored the gnawing suggestion that perhaps he should have planned this particular exercise with as much detail as his retirement of the website.

Nadine featured in his daydreams about the impact of a new look of course. David was self-aware enough to acknowledge his own arrogance, and also the fact that the change of image might possibly improve his love-life opportunities. He was too old for a pony tail, as he'd heard to his cost. The potential improvement to his appearance and desirability was rooted in an optimism which he didn't really believe was founded in reality, but it was a thought to hang on to. A positive. As more hair fell to the floor around him, David allowed a small pang of regret to echo around his rapidly lighter-feeling skull. Despite all of the difficulties and unforeseen twists to the website adventure, he'd really enjoyed being the Man in the Bath for as long as the good times had lasted, and sharing his thoughts with the world. Sharing, and having them taken notice of. It was one thing to have the opinions, but he couldn't deny the feelgood factor of people looking up to you as well, and respecting those opinions. No, not just respecting… following and believing. And whatever else, he *had* made a difference to some people, hadn't he?

"It'll take a bit of getting used to, won't it boss?"

David nodded absently; his eyes closed. It shouldn't take any getting used to, really. In reality, it wasn't much of a change, or a loss. It was simply going back to what he'd been before, and he'd been happy before, hadn't he? Maybe he wouldn't stay in the same job, though. That was one thing he'd learned. All those trivial things about the job that he used to enjoy were now just an irritation. And he'd need a new project. Something to occupy him, to take his mind off this fiasco. He could even move. Go back to Penrith, perhaps? David had stayed in Leeds after doing his degree, and had never seriously considered relocating again until now. Now seemed like a good time. There were colleges back in the Lakes, and he should have no problem in getting a job with his experience; there were even Universities. Every former college was a University now, it seemed.

Gradually, the radio in the background floated into his consciousness. It was a presenter making the usual inane comments between records, but already the news was obviously out. With his eyes closed he listened through the sound of the scissors.

"... so this one goes out to our favourite Mint B, the 'Man in the Bath,' we'll miss you big fella, and hopefully you'll be back soon..."

And the sounds of Louis Armstrong followed, duetting with Gary Crosby on a track about fishing.

David's brow furrowed, a little mystified by the choice of song, but happy enough that the news had broken, and people knew that the Man in the Bath was no more, even if some of them were hoping he'd return. He settled back into the chair to enjoy the music. David liked Satchmo.

Chp 21 – Retirement

There were numerous odd looks and double-takes, and more than one comment though thankfully, most of the reactions seemed to be a mixture of surprise and approval. Elias had given his best attempt at a compliment, but with his distinctly shaky social skills, it hadn't been phrased in the best of terms.

"You don't look like a sasquatch anymore."

It brought a smile now as he remembered the hesitant expression on the professor's face, as though waiting for approval for that astute observation. David hadn't taken offence. Professor Cornwell hadn't intended to compliment, but as David's superior he didn't have to. His reaction had been a grunting approval, with a muttering along the lines that it was about time he'd smartened himself up. The best reaction had been the smile without words from Nadine, which he took as a tacit approbation, just as he'd hoped it might. David had risked a speculative question, to find out if she'd been going to the usual Friday after-works drinks, and the simple 'I'll be there' contained just enough warmth that he could imagine their friendship was back on track.

"Excuse me, could I ask you a question please. If you have a moment?"

It was a timid, scruffy, student who carried her books under one arm, at scientifically improbable angles. David grinned and opened his door.

"Of course. Come in and take a seat."

Those words sounded wonderfully comforting to his own ears, and he strode round the desk with a renewed vigour. Today it was good to be back, doing what he did best. Dr Dunn sat down in his chair and smiled, toying with the top of a blue biro. The job didn't seem so bad after all.

"So what can you do for me today?"

The girl hesitated, lowered her eyes, then smiled, remembering the administrator's well known idiosyncratic greeting.

"I'm having problems with the finance office. They say I haven't paid my fees but... if you remember... you sent them a letter..."

David interjected happily.

"Yes, yes, of course... Sarah, isn't it? Let me just have a look at my records, and I'll get them on the phone and straighten it out for you..."

#

The rumour must have started mid-morning, but the first time it made its way to his ears was on the short walk to the staff cafeteria at lunchtime. At first it was just caught phrases from groups of students muttering excitedly, phrases like 'it's back,' and 'he's back.' A shiver ran down David's spine, and he immediately thought about 'The Man.' Shaking the sensation off and telling himself not to be so paranoid, he'd made his way through the outlying building, ears straining to catch other words. But he heard nothing more.

He was slightly more composed by the time he reached the food counter, greeting the staff with his usual smile and order, and spotting Nadine sat alone at the far round corner table. She noticed him too, and beckoned him over, lifting David's spirits and filling him with new optimism. He paid quickly, not bothering about the loose change he was due, and hurried over to the table, where he was greeted with a warm and affectionate smile.

"Hi. I'm glad you're here..."

The words were wonderful to hear, and took all thoughts of the gossip away. He opened his mouth to return the greeting, but was cut off mid-sentence.

"I've been waiting for someone to tell. I heard some of the students talking, and it's true apparently. The 'Man in the Bath' is back. Just a technology problem apparently. He's back. We've still got him!"

The sight of her beaming mouth coincided with an icy sensation running right down David's spine. His mouth opened and closed a couple of times wordlessly.

"...still got him?"

Nadine mistook this for excitement.

"I know. Fantastic, isn't it? I was worried something had happened to him. Something bad... you know... it always happens to the innovators and the great orators... you know, Dr King... JFK... but he's back!"

Sweat was instantly dripping down under his armpits, and he could feel the colour drain from his face while he tried to comprehend what was going on. A month earlier, he'd have been delighted and highly amused to be compared to Kennedy and Martin Luther King. Now, it brought on a terror that someone as educated as Dr Nadine Silk could even utter the suggestion.

"... you're sure he's back... I mean... it's not just a copycat...?"

She shook her head animatedly, sipping on her coffee and leaning forwards conspiratorially, pausing to glance down, as though she'd just noticed her blouse was unbuttoned at the top. She smiled once more and leaned lower in a deliberately affected way.

"No... that's what I thought at first too, but the whole site is back, all of it, word for word... he just apologises for what he says was a temporary lapse in service. Says he had to change servers, whatever a server is... that the original provider wasn't 'providing' anymore, so there's now a new 'provider'... I don't know what it all means, I'm rubbish at computer stuff as you well know, but isn't it great?"

David's mind was racing and very quickly hit the brakes when it came to him that the admin had already been hacked once, before, when 'The Priest' had deleted the fake identity he'd posted under. So whoever this 'Priest' was, he would have had the opportunity to download everything from the site's administrator tools.

"Everything...? What about the last message? The one where he said he was leaving? For good?"

Nadine shrugged, leaning back, and tossing her hair.

"I don't know anything about that... sounds like a hoax to me... I feel like celebrating. Do you fancy doing something later? Something decadent?"

The offer, which would have had him salivating and panting like a puppy only twenty minutes earlier, now barely even registered. And the cold sweats increased. The site was back, but he didn't even know where it was, much less have any control over it. Whoever had done this now had total control over what was said. And *the original provider wasn't 'providing' any more so there was a new 'provider.'* It was cryptic, but David couldn't help feeling that it was a message directly to him.

"Has... has he appeared again yet? Made another video?"

It was a nervous question, which again Nadine mistook for excitement.

"Not yet, not when I looked. It's really hit you too, hasn't it? I can't believe it, something like this making me feel like a little schoolgirl again... we could... you could come round after work if you liked, bring a bottle of wine, and we could log on and wait for it together if you wanted... so long as you don't mind me acting like an excited little schoolgirl that is..."

Nadine's cheeks were slightly pink and she leaned forwards to flash her cleavage, but David didn't notice that. He was looking at her angrily.

"For God's sake, grow up Nadine! It's a website. It's some idiot with nothing better to do talking crap. You can't actually believe in it!"

Her expression changed instantly. Her face took on cold, angular lines.

"Jealousy is an ugly thing... And forget about tonight. You've ruined my mood. Your loss."

And she got up and stalked away haughtily.

Chp 22 – I'm Spartacus

It couldn't go on. The movement, the 'Community,' was growing faster than ever before, and now it seemed that 'The Priest' had taken on the status of figurehead and spokesperson. Whole new sections had been added to the site, which scarily advocated action, as well as thought. Other people might not have noticed, but some of the existing sections had been carefully edited too, retrospectively changing some messages just enough to alter the tone. And the media seemed to have taken up the cause, with two of the tabloids even running a comment section, updating those without access to the web on the latest posts.

David made a decision. It might cost him his job but he couldn't just stand by and watch what was happening, which was why he tidied himself up and made a phone call, to a contact in the local news office. And was why he found himself sitting in a chair in a news studio four hours later, waiting to go live.

#

Presenter: And so, onto our final piece, and something I think you might all find of interest. The Daily News was contacted today by a well-respected academic from the University with some shocking news. With the story, and with Dr David Dunn, our political correspondent, Michael Check.

It wasn't a bad introduction, but David could feel himself starting to shake. It had taken the pulling of several strings, and a number of favours to get this appearance, despite objections from the station management, but whatever it took, he was determined to finally set the record straight.

Michael Check: Good evening. Tonight, we have an unusual story and one that I must say, despite my professional objectivism, that I'm slightly embarrassed to be presenting. In the studio we have Dr David Dunn, who controversially claims to be the famed 'Man in the Bath,' and who also alleges that the movement, 'The Community,' as it is commonly known, and of which many of you are members, have been duped by an elaborate practical joke. Something which I personally feel to be in extremely poor taste. So, Dr Dunn, lets start with the obvious… even with the distortion, you look nothing like the character we know and love from the screen…

David felt the cold terror returning and clenched his fists, trying desperately not to sweat. Very aware that he hadn't thought this through enough, and hadn't properly prepared for the most mundane and obvious of questions he would inevitably be asked.

Dr Dunn: Thank you Michael… errr… well, as you're obviously familiar with the video clips you'll know that I pixelated my face as I wanted to retain my anonymity. The only thing different about me now, is that I've had my hair cut. If you ask anyone who knew me a few weeks ago or show a photo you'll see that…

Michael Check: Lets move on from the physical resemblance then, although despite the attempts at covering up, you'll be well aware that a number of scientists have reconstructed the likely face and if I may say, it isn't yours… let's move on to your point there about anonymity… if you didn't want to be recognised when your audience numbered in the hundreds, why come out now that millions watch you.

David coughed, and picked up his glass to wet his lips, unable to stop the shaking of his hand that threatened to spill the water.

Dr Dunn: Sorry… I'm nervous, I've never been on TV before…

Michael Check: That doesn't seem to bother the 'Man in the Bath,' with his audience of millions worldwide.

Dr Dunn: That's not fair. That isn't live!

David winced at his own petulant tone, starting to wish that he had thought of some other way to reveal the truth. A written article for a newspaper perhaps, which would have given him time to present his arguments at his own, considered pace.

Michael Check: Let's cut to the chase, Dr Dunn. Isn't this just a scam to try and claim credit for a profitable, worldwide enterprise? To raise your profile by claiming the insights and wisdom of another?

Dr Dunn: Of course not! And I've never made a penny out of it. And while you mention it, they're hardly insights or wisdom… I mean, there's some wisdom there of course, but it's just my thoughts on things…

The sentence tailed off quite pathetically. This wasn't going as intended at all.

Michael Check: So you're claiming that the site means nothing, regardless of your claims to writing it? Are you saying that something believed in by thousands… millions of people… is nothing more than a joke?

Dr Dunn: Well, not a joke exactly. But it isn't exactly serious either. It's just… just my thoughts…

For someone who prided himself on the flow of his stream of consciousness monologues, David was feeling distinctly disjointed. And was acutely aware that it showed. He saw the twitch in the interviewer's mouth and should have predicted the next question.

Michael Check: If I may say so Dr Dunn, you don't exactly show any of the eloquence or insight that appears in *your* clips…

The second to last words were heavily emphasized, and David couldn't help but notice the pointedly raised eyebrow towards the camera.

Dr Dunn: As I said, I'm not used to such a large, live audience, but I can assure you that everything I'm saying is true. I'd be more than happy to take a polygraph, or have experts analyse my voice to compare to the clips I posted.

A wry thought occurred, as he tried to ignore the bead of sweat slowly trickling from his left armpit down his side under his shirt. As a polygraph is based on physical reactions and partly on sweating, then he'd probably fail.

Michael Check: And you say that the site isn't meant to be serious. What about all of the people who follow the words and directions religiously, that find solace and guidance in the words of the Man in the Bath? Are you mocking the loyal Community, Dr Dunn? Is it just a joke to you?

Dr Dunn: Not a joke exactly, I mean no, of course not, it's just that it doesn't mean as much to me as it does to them. For me, it started out as a kind of… hobby I guess… you could say that some of it was jokey… but not at the expense of my viewers, I might add. As it grew, it became less funny. And people shouldn't follow what someone else thinks. I said that on my site!

Several more beads of sweat had joined the first and were in process of forming a small river down his side, which he hoped didn't show through the shirt. And it was just about this point that David realised that there was nothing he could say that was likely to rescue this car crash of an interview, and that he needed to do something fairly drastic if he was to have any hope at all of rescuing the situation.

Michael Check: Actually Dr Dunn, what the 'Man in the Bath' said, was that people shouldn't follow the words of men if they didn't know where they came from. He explicitly stated that in religions such as Islam or Judaism he had no issue, and actually supported the following of the word of God. It was only in the case where an unknown man or men had written the words of instruction that we should be wary.

Dr Dunn: I'm not God! And the site isn't words of instruction. And anyway, that would be exactly my point, you *don't* know who wrote it!

He recognised the trap as soon as the words left his lips.

Michael Check: But you're saying that *you* wrote the words Dr Dunn, so we <u>do</u> know who wrote them, don't we? And I can't possibly agree that the Man in the Bath doesn't provide instruction. Didn't he specifically provide a guide towards enlightenment? Doesn't he explicitly guide people on what they should, and shouldn't, do? If you're the author as you claim, you should know this!

It was a cheap shot, but not one that any rational retort could overcome. David struggled with the cuff of his shirt, and started to roll the sleeve up, as quickly as possible.

Dr David Dunn: Look… you seem to know so much about my site you must know what this is?

He pushed the cuff up as high as it would go, but with the tightness of the material around his arm, the shirt sleeve only exposed the skin up to just above the elbow, showing nothing. David started to blush. He reached for the buttons of his shirt, dislodging the microphone clip, which dropped to the floor with a crackle.

Michael Check: Well I think that's all the time we have, I'm afraid. Thank you for coming into the studio.

The look of disgust on the interviewer's face was plain, and David's words were lost without a microphone, even as he explained what he was trying to do, struggling to unbutton his shirt to show off the tattoo at the top of his arm. The unique, self-designed tattoo (a previous project) was the proof that would verify his identity from the videos, and verify that he was unequivocally who David claimed he was.

"And we're out..."
The floor manager's words came before he'd managed three buttons. And without even looking over at his guest, Michael Check got up from his seat and hurried away. David just sat there, forlorn, half undressed. The colour rose to his cheeks as he looked around and found not a single person was meeting his gaze. It took every ounce of strength to hold back the tears of humiliation.

Chp 23 – Back in Business

He phoned in sick once more the next day. There was no other option, really. There was only so much humiliation you could face in one week, and the number one priority for Dr David Dunn was to vindicate himself. Which was proving to be far more problematic than originally anticipated, and which needed time to effectively plan and develop.

He stood in the doorway to the bathroom, cradling a hot cup of coffee in his red 'I Love Paris' mug, mulling over the problem. The central problem was that David had been far too thorough when excising every trace of the original 'Man in the Bath.' His eyes roamed around the room, over the sink, over the fresh magnolia paint, and the already peeling wallpaper reaching up for a metre above the rim of the bath.

In addition to cutting his hair after seemingly closing the site for good, on the same day, David had enjoyed a cathartic afternoon, redecorating. The blue and white tiles had been quite literally and messily ripped off the walls, necessitating the current, temporary, wallpaper. The original white, matte paint on the walls had been covered up by a new magnolia look, without even bothering to rub down first, hence the rather patchy current colour scheme.

He sipped the hot coffee as he remembered that afternoon and evening, burning his tongue in the process, which seemed to be a frequent occurrence these days, and barely registered any more. One of those obsessions he frequently experienced had crept into his mind as he'd redecorated his bathroom, and had forced its way deep into his psyche. As the contents of the wine bottle had sunk lower that evening, so his obsession had increased too. Leaving the broken and cracked tiles on the floor, he'd returned to his computers, and had used an erasing program to remove all traces of 'The Man in the Bath' from the laptop. And then from his desktop. Next, a hammer and pair of pliers had been utilised in the back yard, to totally remove all backup traces from the silver discs he meticulously kept. Even the original years-old video files had been mercilessly butchered until nothing remained. David had even considered laser removal of his own tattoo, but fortunately it had been well past the last cocktail hour by then, and the idea had been put on hold till the next day, when a hangover and common sense had prevailed. That next morning had meant the removal of the detritus from the bomb-site of a bathroom, and the purchasing of paint and wallpaper to regain some semblance of order. The decorating had taken place under a thinly disguised fug of guilt at what he'd done. But he'd wanted, needed, every trace of the Man in the Bath, removed from his life. The site had gone, he'd retired, and he didn't want even the slightest reminder.

David sipped the coffee as he surveyed the bombsite of a bathroom, all helpful proof that this truly was the background of his videos now gone.

"So... technically... I'm a bit buggered..."

David spoke out loud softly, to no-one in particular. In the background, his mind was working on possible methods of salvaging the situation, and a half-formed plan was silently evolving, in opposition to his negative words.

Sober and more rational today, calmed by his removal from company, and from the thoughts and words of others, this was turning into a challenge. And one thing Dr David Dunn liked was a challenge. Hence the new plan.

#

"Hi, Man in the Bath here... I apologise for having let matters continue in the hands of others, and I genuinely did intend my retirement to be permanent, but I'm afraid I had to come back, just to set everyone straight, and stop you all being taken advantage of…"

David felt incredibly nervous. He wasn't quite sure why this should be different from any other video-clip, but today he felt awkward, and was afraid it was going to show, despite the regulation pixelated face.

"I shut down the site because… because you're all pricks…"

He sat there for a moment, staring into the camera.

"Bollocks."

Leaving the video running, David settled back, and closed his eyes.

"This is harder than I thought it would be… all I wanted to do was come on here and tell the truth but… how do you actually do that…? How do I convince you that I really am who I say I am? And that I stopped doing this because you're all idiots, who don't know a good thing when you've got it?"

David opened his eyes again.

"I guess I could just not pixelate. Let everyone see me for real, see who I actually am, physically? That could work… though you never actually saw me in the first place, did you? So perhaps that's not the best idea. And after that television debacle… how do you pronounce that in English by the way... day bark...? dib harkle...? If I've ever used the word on here before you'll probable notice I kind of mumble it... bugger, not really the time to go off on a tangent really, is it...? Maybe I should just go back to how it was... maybe I should post this as it is, so you can see my thought processes... then maybe you'd recognize me? If I'd kept the originals, I could do that with all of my videos but..."

David suppressed a giggle.

"...but I'm a fucking idiot too, and I deleted them all in a hissy fit... hoist' by my own petard I guess... interesting phrase that... I used to know what it meant..."

A frown wrinkled his brow.

"...no... I'm not getting started like that again... or maybe I should, just to show I'm who I say I am... oh bollocks..."

He sank lower into the bath until his head was submerged, and held his breath for as long as he could, coming up with a gasp of air and pressing his short hair flat to his head, to drain the water off.

"This needs some more thought... this is the Man in the Bath, probably needing to buy a fake wig in order to be convincing, now going to the pub, and putting the immersion heater back on, to try this again later..."

The Saint was sitting alone in The Owl House, nursing half a pint of Guinness, and he gestured David to join him with a welcoming smile, which was a bit of a surprise, though in a good way. David nodded acceptance, and ordered himself a Jack Daniels on the rocks, making a mental note that he shouldn't drink too much as he had more important tasks to complete later, ones that needed relative sobriety.

"Hi Dave, how's it going?"

David shrugged, trying to ignore the flushes he felt rising in his cheeks and the tenseness in his shoulders, knowing the elephant in the room would need to be addressed, sooner or later.

"Not too bad. Yourself?"

He feigned relaxation as he sat down, first crossing his legs awkwardly, then uncrossing them again, realising that the body language would betray him.

"What have you been up to?"

"Decorating..."

There was a painful silence of indeterminate length as David wished, as hard as he could, that Saint would just get it out of the way, and mention the interview outright. The figure opposite just smiled back though, with an expression that hinted at sympathy. After another thirty or so long, silent, seconds, interspersed with glances around the pub and sips at drinks, David let his shoulders slump. He may as well get it over with himself.

"I guess you heard about the TV thing?"

It was an unexpected sensation, but just saying it out loud was like a heavy weight lifting. Saint grinned that peculiar lopsided grin of his, and chuckled.

"Didn't hear about it, watched it. You made a right tit of yourself!"

David couldn't help laughing himself, at the innocent frankness of the remark.

"You could say that."

He raised his whisky glass in salute, and Saint returned the gesture, brushing his fringe back over his pale forehead.

"What the fuck did you do that for?"

It was strange. One on one, Saint seemed like quite a different person. It took a moment's examination of memory to realise that they'd genuinely never had a private social conversation, in all the time they'd been working together. Not just the two of them. And surprisingly, it felt quite comfortable. David felt the compulsion to be totally honest.

"Desperation... I honestly didn't know what else to do."

"Did you mean all the things you said on there? About it not being serious?"

David sucked air between his lips as he considered.

"Yes, but I didn't phrase it very well, did I?"

"You think?"

It was quite odd, but David had the distinct feeling from the question that the validity of him being the authentic Man in the bath Wasn't an issue here, and wasn't even in doubt. It was such a relief not to have to defend something as seemingly undefendable as the truth, do David wasn't going to raise that matter himself.

"But now I'm in a bit of a fix. The interview has kind of... fucked it up a bit more... and... I've been decorating..."

A raised eyebrow indicated that he should carry on.

"... when it all got... a bit much... I decided to 'kill' the Man off... but as suicide isn't my style, I decided to kill everything around him instead... distance myself from it totally... took the site down, deleted everything, and changed my bathroom completely from what shows on the videos... very badly as it happens..."

A wry, trademark 'Man in the Bath' grin.

"... which means that when someone hijacked the site and put it back up... some git called 'The Priest' apparently, I now have no means of proving who I genuinely am... I made all that effort to make myself unidentifiable... then made all the effort to remove all traces of it... and now I need to prove that this new bastard isn't me... Catch 22..."

It sounded lame, even to his own ears.

"Why do you want to?"

"Because..."

Now this was more difficult to explain truthfully. If you don't mention vanity and wounded pride as part of the reason, then it sounds completely implausible, so given the scale of the potential answer, David opted for partial truth.

"Originally, it was just a bit of fun... and for a while I did seem to make a difference to some people... which was great too, and I did probably take it a bit more seriously then..."

He was very aware of Saint's grey eyes studying him closely, and felt a little embarrassed, trying to balance humility with pride.

"...but anyway, too many people got the wrong idea from what I was saying, and it took on a life of its own... you've seen some of the things that have happened in my name..."

He winced at the phrase, realising he must be coming across as even more arrogant than he actually was.

"... people using what I said as fact rather than opinion... doing... bad things... people... people died, Simon..."

He couldn't find any more words to describe his horror further. There was a hot flush in his cheeks, and for the first time he could remember in recent history, David wanted to let himself cry.

"...I guess I felt guilty too... like those things were actually my fault...."

"Weren't they? You did write and say those things, didn't you?"

The tacit admission that he was who he said was overwhelmed by the implication that the blame really might lie at his own feet. Or in his own bath, at least. David blinked back the wetness he could sense starting to well, in the corner of one eye.

"...some of them, but I didn't mean... I didn't want anyone to take me at my words, or I wouldn't have been so... facetious..."

The sentence trailed off lamely.

"But you did want people to listen and take notice, didn't you? Wasn't that the point?"

The only answer to that was to drain the glass and offer to buy another round. There was a blackness descending to the conversation, but David didn't want it to end. Irrationally, admitting his own faults out loud helped to diminish them. He pondered that, as he stood at the bar, ordering. When he got back to the table, he had to ask the question.

"...so... do you believe me? Really?"

Saint shrugged.

"Does it matter? You obviously believe it... I believe *that*..."

There wasn't no answer to that. Not a good one anyway. David sighed, and took a mouthful of whisky.

"Can't you... don't you worry about the craziness of it all... as a... as an intelligent, impartial observer... don't you worry about how everyone seems totally taken in?

It was Simon's turn to shrug, though his penetrating eyes never left David's face.

"People believe what they want to... people are stupid... they believe what they want to believe..."

"Do you..."

The hairs on the back of his neck prickled, and he couldn't meet that gaze, staring down at the oak table holding the drinks instead.

"Did you ever log on? Yourself? What did you... think about it...?"

David didn't notice the eyes turn away from him.

"Why don't you just let it go, David..."

#

"Hi, this is the 'Man in the Bath'... I'm back..."

Slightly more relaxed from the whiskies, he allowed himself a pause, trying to get his head back into the same frame of mind he'd used for the previous takes, earlier in the day.

"Sorry I've been away, and I apologise for the slight alteration in décor..."

His hand swung out to show the freshly tiled backdrop, and repainted walls above.

"But I fancied a change... you should try it... same goes for the barnet..."

David rubbed his short hair vigorously, and then steepled his fingers in some scooped up foam.

"I just came back to warn you that I seem to have a fan... not like yourself... I have a stalker, an impersonator if you will... in short, some total bastard has stolen my website!"

This allowed for another hopefully recognisable, trademark dramatic pause. The more trademark moves in this video the better.

"I took the original down myself because... well, I've been trying to think of the best way to say this without ruining all of my previously sterling work in educating the great unwashed… which was why I originally chose to do this from the bath, by the way…”

David beamed despite his nervousness, extremely pleased with that turn of phrase, which had just popped into his head, even though it was a blatant lie.

“But… some of the Community… some of my Community, I guess… weren't quite as balanced as I'd hoped… no, sorry, balanced isn't fair… let's just say they grasped the wrong end of the nettle… I don't blame them… human nature is as human nature does, as my mother used to say… but this brings me back to the subject of my lesson for today my children… human nature, and how the best intentions, in this case mine, can be subverted by others, by human nature itself.”

David felt more comfortable this second time attempting the video. It was unclear if it was just because of the whisky, talking openly to Simon, the relief of finally tackling the subject head-on, or the no doubt relaxing properties of a second foam bath in one day.

“I'm afraid that today, my friends, I have to reveal to you a fundamental truth which I'd previously shielded you from… that in essence, and to use the title of today's little talk, people are scum..."

The fingers steepled, carefully. This was a tricky subject, but if handled with care might solve, or at the very least ease, many of the problems in David's mind.

"Now I know what you're going to say... the milk of human kindness, the underlying goodness of people, Samaritans or otherwise, our selfless charity to those less fortunate, all of those things large and small, that people do just to make others feel good... but that's all bollocks, as I've recently discovered to my own personal cost. So, I thought it was about time I came clean, to coin a phrase... which is why you can today see me in all my less-than-glory, pixilation and distortion-free!"

David picked up the soap and started to work up a lather in his palms while he talked.

"But I'm wandering somewhat. You may have noticed that I do that quite often. What I need people to know is...the fact of the matter, my friends, is that you've been duped. This might sound a little difficult to comprehend but I'm afraid my site, and my views, have been hi-jacked..."

He paused. This was the really tricky bit. Whether to admit that his views had been hi-jacked by the audience he was addressing now, and how to sugar that pill appropriately. Chickening out, he ignored the question completely, and left the claim ambiguous.

"When I took my site down recently, retired it and myself, someone took it upon themselves to carry on my work, without my consent, or approval. The site that is currently running under my normal title is a fake, copied from the original and uploaded when I retired. Now normally, I wouldn't mind this too much. One of the reasons I started was to make people think for themselves, but this act, and the fact that the current administrator doesn't seem to adhere to my principles, or real views, means that I have to return from my early retirement with this warning. Please don't be fooled by imposters. I'm sure that you're all intelligent, and are aware enough to recognise the real me now, and do feel free to compare my voice, my tattoo, my speech patterns if you're uncertain... but as I said, some people subvert thoughts, and twist them to their own ends. I don't know what the imposter is going to do, but for God's sake, don't give him any money or believe what he says. He's scum..."

David soaped his shoulders and sank under the warm water to rinse them off, vaguely aware of a strange déjà vu sensation, but putting the feeling down to a familiarity of the subject matter.

"Which, as I mentioned, is the subject of today's address... I'm returning for a little while, and you're lucky enough to be able to see one final, genuine, Man in the Bath talk... so... people are scum..."

He smiled as sweetly as he could manage at the camera.

"Let's look at the facts, and examine together the deeper nature of the human animal, with all of his many flaws, all of his achievements, all of his possibilities and potential, and what he chooses to do with them..."

David lifted a hand to show the flattening white bubbles disappearing from the chemical reaction with the soap. A slushy ring of residue showed itself on back of his hand.

"... scum..."

#

It was midnight by the time he managed to get the new website live. The original name wasn't available any more of course, and many of the similar ones had already gone so, after some deliberation David had located and settled on TheOriginalManinBath.com, close enough to be able to get accidental hits, with a number of links inserted and meta descriptions to attract web-bots.

The website wasn't stunning by any means and was a relatively sparse affair, with a photograph of his recognisable tattoo centre page, and a brief explanation of what had happened, next to a link to the new video clip. Original logo of course, reconstructed as best he could. Every form of protection from hacking he could find had been purchased and applied to the site.

David sat in the office chair staring at the computer screen, wishing there was someone he could call and tell. But the only two people who sprang to mind were Liz, and Nadine. For some reason, he felt he would be more comfortable conversing with a woman about this whole affair. But he didn't phone anyone. In the real world, he wasn't likely to get the reception he needed, from either of them.

#

TheOriginalManinBath.com had disappeared within six hours. The protection he'd applied to the website was clearly useless. In its stead, if you tried the URL, was a placeholder with big letters naming one Dr David Dunn as a fake and a fraud, and giving his genuine real-world address, claiming this was part of a new, popular movement to 'name and shame' those who brought the 'Man in the Bath' into disrepute.

In his private e-mail inbox was an e-message that made David's heart initially leap in hope, listed as being from the Barechested_Princess. The elation lasted only as long as it took to open the body of the text.

You are the scum! I happen to know the real Man in the Bath, and your feeble attempts at copycat messages would be funny, if they weren't so sick. You should at least do a little research before trying something that stupid. The Man forgives you for what you've done, but I do not. That is why we, of the Community, have chosen to name and shame people like you, in the hope that is discourages others from taking his name, or identity, in vain. He is a great man, and if you took the time to listen to his words, instead of showing your jealousy through petty acts such as this, you might find yourself a better person.
You've been warned, Dr David Dunn. We all know who you are, and any further attempts at claiming His identity will result in severe repercussions. The Priesthood will no longer tolerate your interference.

David's heart was pounding by the time he came to the end of the message. And it started to thump even faster when he noticed the next mail.

From: <u>The_Priest@hotmail.co.uk</u>
To: <u>David.Dunn@Holbeckuniversity.ac.uk</u>
Subject: The Man In The Bath

Dear David,

It is your own fault. You have betrayed the cause. I would just like you to be aware just how easy it would be for me to destroy your life right now.

I won't destroy you though, as I and The Community owe you thanks for first creating the idea of the Man In The Bath. As we both know, ideas are powerful things, David, but you are a fool, a hypocrite, and a traitor to your own words.

I was one of the first to follow you, to believe in you, to trust in you, back in the days before the Word was spread. You were special, and will always hold a dear place in our hearts, for allowing us to have our Voice heard.

The symbol is more important than any one man, Dr Dunn.

I am a reasonable person, as you know, and I have given you every opportunity to continue leading our crusade. You have been found wanting. Other members of The Community are less tolerant than I, but I hold sway. I may be lenient, but I will not allow you to destroy the beautiful thing you have created.

Perhaps you should just fade into the background. Let it go. It would be the wise move on your part.

This isn't going away. It's time to move things up a gear, David.

Ps. Please don't get any silly ideas about this message. The e-mail address I'm using is registered in your name, with your own details. No-one will believe you.

Chp 26 – Sacked

"Everything... has gone to shiiiiiit!"
David Dunn screamed up at the grey skies, slurring his words slightly. No-one was around to watch him, and that was exactly the reason he'd got the bus out to Roundhay Park, and walked to the most deserted area he knew. And it was such a release, just to get all of the anger and frustration out.

"To SHIIIIIITTTTT!!!!"
David found himself gasping for breath from the exertion. He rested his hands on his knees and bent forwards, panting, feeling guilty for being so out of shape, but gearing up for another bout of screaming.

"You're all... FUCKING SCUUUMMMMM!"

#

The day had started normally, which these days meant badly, and had gone rapidly downhill from there. To start with, he'd had another thumping hangover. Though these were now becoming the norm, and no longer bothered him that much. Even the messy evacuation of the bowels that came shortly after getting up was more of a relief than an annoyance or worry.

Dry toast had followed, along with the customary large mug of coffee, laced with a little rum, just to take the edge off. He'd sat on the green fabric couch, ignoring the television. It wasn't switched on. Couldn't be switched on. It was probably time he upgraded to a modern television anyway, rather than this obsolete, cathode-ray tube, version. Which didn't work.

Three days earlier, a news special on the now global phenomenon of the Man in the Bath had precipitated an ornamental thick glass ashtray coming into speedy contact with the screen. It still lay on the floor amidst the shards of glass, having eventually fallen from where it was embedded of its own accord. Even that action had been a disappointment, though. Rather than the fireworks and explosion he had expected from cinematic experiences of tv destruction, there had been a pop, a few sparks, and a smell of burnt ozone. David had carefully skirted around the large screen, wary that a delayed reaction might injure him in retaliation for, his fit of pique, and had switched off the socket before removing the plug. The destruction remained as a monument to the realisation that nothing he could do was going to stop the juggernaut to which he'd given birth, although it barely resembled what he'd originally created any more. It was abstract. He was moving through the events of the day in a detached frame of mind, as that seemed the only way to survive and cope. His whole life seemed little more than a movie itself. Events that happened. Weren't real. Fiction.

Dressed and travelling to work, and only thirty minutes late, all he'd heard were whispers and drifting media reports, nothing to take him out of this nightmare, the Orwellian nightmare of his own making. The world gone mad. How could no-one notice? How could he be the only one not to fall under the miasma? David had wanted to laugh. Halfway to work, he <u>had</u> laughed out loud, without meaning to. A wild cackle of a laugh, bringing concerned stares and eye-avoidance. That had just made him laugh even more.

Then he'd noticed the whispers. People weren't just talking about the site. A sly glance here, a tilt of the head there and suddenly it was clear that Dr David Dunn was far from anonymous. The low rumble of paranoia that escaped around his brain suggested that he was far from popular as well. And it wasn't just paranoia any more, was it? It was actually happening, for real.

By the service station, he'd stood and gawped upwards at the twenty foot billboard hoarding, berating people who didn't see 'The Way,' and inviting them to join 'The Community,' and 'See the Light.' David had laughed again. He couldn't help it. He'd thrown his head back, and let out an unfettered, wild cackle of a laugh, reminding himself of a silent-movie villain. That had been when everything had exploded.

"You're the fucking scum mate! Listen to the Priest! See sense!"

Only half aware of what was going on, David had propped himself up on his left elbow, and reached up towards his face, wincing at the splitting pain as his fingers came away from his nose with scarlet flecks. David had blinked, winced again as he found that it hurt and brought tears to his eyes, and looked up at the shadow towering over him.

He'd quickly hidden the mirth that threatened to show. The owner of the fist that had punished his laugh could have been no older than fifteen, but the dark expression across the boy's features suggested that levity would have been the worst possible reaction. It had taken a fraction of a second too long for David to realise that the momentary upward curl of his own lip had been noted, and about two seconds until the delayed reaction of the training shoe connecting between his legs registered.

David heard a mournful howl as he curled up involuntarily into a ball, not knowing it came from his own mouth. He'd barely noticed when the glob of spit hit the back of his bare neck.

"That's for pretending to be Him, you twat... you'd better start to wise up, Mister... before it's too late..."

He'd lain there, curled into a ball, unmoving and silent except for the heavily panting breaths, listening to the footfalls moving past.

#

A mirror in the toilet of McDonald's had revealed that the damage wasn't too severe, and red-faced from the shame more than anything, David had forcefully blanked everything out of his mind as he carefully cleaned his face, and gingerly examined himself for any further damage elsewhere. He exited the shop slowly, eyes flashing left and right, and limping a little. The sky seemed oppressive and David sensed danger in every face, and every painful step of the way.

The feeling receded only slightly by the time he reached the campus of the University, but the real sideways glances continued. The hostility. It was a surreal experience, particularly passing the glass-fronted Faculty lounge, where David had to stop and watch, seeing his now infamous interview being replayed in a silent montage, watched by a rapt audience staring at the TV mounted on the wall. Subtitles flashed up onto the screen between a number of talking heads, all recognisable faces from around the world, and all seemingly talking about the 'Man in the Bath.' There were soundbites and subtitled quotations, mostly completely out of context, taken from a number of his own posts and videos. He'd seen them before. You couldn't avoid them on the news now. Licking his painful lips, David tried to rack his brains to identify some of the soundbite quotes that didn't even seem like they'd come from him.

Two girls whispering loudly brought his attention back to the present, and David pulled his long coat tighter around himself, striding briskly off towards the Liberal Arts Department building.

Once inside, David closed the door firmly and exhaled a long, slow sigh of relief that he was finally alone. His head seemed to be buzzing, and not only from the punch and the kick. His legs felt weak, and he had to grip the edge of the desk to keep to his feet, as he staggered around to sit in the blue, adjustable chair. His shaking fingers flicked on the kettle, and he pressed the power button on the computer, loosening the coat and slipping it off his shoulders and over the back of the chair. He closed his eyes and sighed.

There were any number of jobs which needed doing today. After his absences he was quite behind with the paperwork, and there were a number of student registration issues and finance queries which already knew needed processing. No doubt there were many more since he'd been here last. It was something tangible to focus on, to ground his screaming brain back in the flesh world again. No introspection, no loose thoughts, no 'Man in the Bath.' Just mechanical work.

Feeling his heartbeat slow slightly, David stood and moved his coat to the customary hook on the wall, where it really belonged, pulling open the windows and spooning a large, heaped amount of coffee and two sugars into his mug, pouring on the water and stirring, fascinated by the swirling liquid and the globules of un-dissolved coffee granules. He chased them round with the spoon for thirty seconds, before settling back down in from of the computer screen.

David typed in his username and password and waited. Then he typed it in again. And then a third time. There was no error message, but no login either.

"Shit!"

The exclamation was louder than he'd intended, as David burned the tip of his tongue on the scalding liquid, sloshing a messy puddle onto his desk while he struggled to put the cup back down safely. He sucked his tongue, dabbing at the spilled coffee with a tissue as he reached for the phone, and dialled IT support, wondering why the ability to drink coffee without scalding himself seemed to have fled entirely. After the customary holding messages, he eventually heard a human voice.

"Hello. This is Dr David Dunn in Liberal Arts. Is there a problem with the network? I can't seem to log on."

There was a pause, and the usual disinterested identity check questions, followed by a long silence. The bland and bored voice at the other end of the telephone suddenly came back sharper, as the operator must have looked at his account and details for the first time.

"Your account has been disabled. You received over 1000 spam e-mail messages, and the automatic software removed your access to the account until it's cleared."

David waited, but no further information was forthcoming.

"So what should I do?"

"Fuck off?"

The answer was quiet and totally deadpan. There was a click, and the line went dead. David sighed, knowing there was no point in getting angry with any computer support. Instead he reached for his in-tray, picking up a small white envelope with his name neatly typed on the front.

Risking another drink of coffee, he tore the envelope open and shook the contents out, into their natural A4 shape.

Dr Dunn,

Yesterday, an extra-ordinary meeting of the Liberal Arts department was held, during which your position was discussed at length. Your behaviour and attitude over recent months have caused significant concerns within the University, and the consensus of the Department is that, in addition to bringing the institution into disrepute by your public actions, your work, attendance record and attitude are completely unacceptable. In addition, I have received a number of complaints from students and staff members about your inappropriate behaviour.

Your position has become untenable, but in recognition of your previous work, I have decided that you may tender your resignation, effective immediately. I expect your letter on my desk by the end of work today.

Professor David Cornwell.

Disbelief soon turned to amusement, and then into anger. This was ridiculous. Insane. His thoughts turned to the possibility that the whole thing was an elaborate prank, then reality hit, and he just knew it was genuine. Quite genuine.

"We'll see about that."

David picked up the telephone, and started to dial the number of the Human Resources department. His fingers stopped. That shouldn't be the first port of call. David reached for the manual records he had of phone numbers, on an old-fashioned piece of paper in his top drawer and found the number for the Union instead. If nothing else, this was totally against all the rules and regulations of the University, and if they wanted a fight, they could have one. He dialled, working out his best approach internally, breathing deeply so as not to appear too angry to whoever answered the phone.

"Geoff...? Oh it's you... great."

David felt a huge swell of relief. It was a familiar voice, which would make this easier. He started by identifying himself, and in the most measured toned he could manage, read out the contents of the letter. Silence followed.

"Well? Come on Geoff, its got to be fucking illegal... or at the least, well out of fucking order."

Another long silence followed, and then an equally measured, level tone of voice.

"You should do what they say…"

"What…?"

Disbelief was all that registered for a moment.

"Come on, stop pissing about, Geoff. I want to do this officially. Official Union business…"

There was another brief pause.

"You should do what they say… and be grateful…"

A click and dead air.

The phone stayed pressed against David's ear, unable to believe what he'd just heard. In the words of the first warning e-mail he'd received, it would be funny, if it wasn't so sick. He pressed a button on the phone to re-dial to Saint's extension, hoping to at least find some sanity left there when it came to his actual job. Panic hadn't set in yet, just disbelief, and he needed a voice he trusted, to tell him if this was indeed just an elaborate and sick hoax. There was no answer so he tried again, for Nadine this time. After six rings there was a pickup.

"Dr Silk…"

"Nadine. Hi, thank God. It's David… Dave…"

A silence followed. An ominous silence that made his heart sink.

"Nadine? It's me. Please, talk to me for a moment. Something bizarre is happening. I've got a message that says I've been sacked."

Another long silence.

"Nadine?"

"If you've been sacked, then you'd better leave."

The tone was cold and emotionless, and it made an anger rise within David's frustrated chest.

"For fuck's sake!"

"... don't contact me again. Ever."

Her tone of voice was level and neutral. Scarily neutral.

"But..."

The phone was put down on the other end of the line, leaving David holding his receiver, open-mouthed. When he finally recovered, something finally snapped inside, and he pushed the mug of coffee slowly forwards along his desk until it toppled onto the floor, making a dull cracking sound as the handle broke off and shot under the bookcase, the remaining brown liquid quickly staining into the cream carpet. David stood, his face a blank mask, and retrieved his coat, walking out and leaving the door unlocked.

He didn't pay any attention to the stares or the surroundings as he wandered home at a leisurely pace, numb. Several car horns went off as he waited to cross the road, paying no attention to the water that sprayed up over his clothes from cars driving deliberately through the lake of dirty water by the kerb. He decided, calmy and logically, to take a route that didn't mean walking next to the open water of the river.

From the end of his road he could already see the bright red paint daubed angrily across his windows and walls. Obscene and threatening words. His brain registered their meaning, but got no reaction. David was beyond reaction. He was back in his movie-verse, moving through the celluloid action, seeing what happened but not a part of it any more. He pushed open the splintered front door and climbed over a broken chair in the hall, heading for the bookcase in the study that would hopefully be intact enough to still hide the half bottle of Jack Daniels.

#

The television channels were swamped. In a daze, and in the absence of a television, he'd used his phone to find the extent of the damage. There were news programmes, special features, histories. You couldn't put your finger on how the escalation had happened, but the 'Man in the

Bath' was literally everywhere. And there was a pervading sense of hope and optimism in every report and conversation. People had bonded over the water cooler, people were chatting on the internet, new social groups were formed in cafés and pubs. The media reported all this, creating yet more talk. The hope, the belief, was that there was a meaning to everything, there was a way to make things better, a path. It was clearer now. There was a way forward. There was a way to a better life. It was so simple. All you had to do was believe. Calmly slipping the whisky bottle into his pocket, David left the house to get the bus to somewhere he could be alone. The most isolated part of the park he could find, far from any other person. He needed to scream at the World.

Chp 27 – The New Clip

He couldn't help logging on. Apart from anything else, he had to see what was being done in his name, and what new humiliation or travesty was being launched. David broke the seal of the bottle, and poured out a large measure of whisky into the glass tumbler with shaking fingers as he clicked the link. He was living in a hotel room now. The laptop was the only thing he'd managed to rescue, and only then because it had been at work with him when his home had been trashed.

On the screen, a familiar scene appeared. A familiar bathroom, a familiar pixelated face, and a familiar tattoo. David wasn't surprised. Nothing surprised him any more.

"Hi, Man in the Bath here…"

The voice was recognisable but not exactly right. It was one of the few things that prevented David from believing he'd gone totally insane.

"Welcome back. As you can see, contrary to some reports I still have all my hair…"

David hit the pause button, staring at the screen. It was perfect. Almost perfect. A frown furrowed his brow, and he racked his brain to see what detail was making it seem very slightly wrong. Abandoning the new clip for now, he navigated his browser back to one of the first video rants, the one on the criminal justice system. He waited for a few nervous seconds, breathing deeply, before going ahead and pressing play.

And there was the original clip, in all its glory. He paid close attention to everything he could see onscreen, and flipped back to the new posting. He confirmed the new visual was definitely David himself, it was certainly him, right down to the previously annoying small crack in the tile, which could be seen above his shoulder on the bathroom wall. He wasn't imagining things, that really was him onscreen. But delivering a new speech that he didn't remember ever making.

Something else was amiss. He searched every corner of the frame on the screen to spot what it might be. Then it hit. Even through the tinny acoustics of the laptop speakers, there was something not quite right about his voice. David slid the volume up, shuffling to get more comfortable on the lumpy, hotel-room bed.

Yes, the voice was definitely wrong. He grimaced, wishing he had his original source files to compare. Like all of us, the sound of his own recorded voice sounded odd to David when played back, and he wanted to compare it to another recording, to make absolutely sure. Twenty seconds later the issue would became redundant. One thing David Dunn knew for certain, and because he was acutely embarrassed about it, was his speech pattern, habit of interjecting, pausing for effect, and repetition. He also knew some of his rants, his favourites, almost off by heart, having the guilty pleasure of having watched them back on numerous occasions, to revel in his own brilliance. He now had a horrible suspicion it wasn't just the administration of the site that was being tampered with.

He navigated the website to the sermon on the genesis of the new testament, his doubts growing by the second, along with a mixture of anticipation and dread. He watched, increasingly slack-jawed, waiting for the moment of absolute proof he was now certain was coming. Onscreen, the figure lifted his chest deliberately out of the water.

"So... the next time the village busybody quotes the Bible at you as God's law, feel free to ask them who wrote the fucking thing in the first place. Personally, I think Jesus might be more than a little pissed off if he was alive today. Here endeth the lesson... so now you know that the Church has been deceiving you, deal with it, don't just accept it ... and next time I might point you in the direction of Christmas, and the birth of Jesus, and make you look up what Yule means before you tuck into your swiss roll Yule Log…"

An icy fear penetrated David's stomach. '*the Church has been deceiving you, deal with it, don't just accept it.*' Those weren't his words. He dragged the slider back to watch again, more carefully this time.

"Damn…"

The whispered exclamation crept from his lips unbidden, and he could hear something approaching admiration in his own voice. It was seamless, with the pixelated face, you couldn't tell at all. That was the genius of course, and by blanking his expressions and mouth, he'd inadvertently made it easy for someone to fake his own videos. And it wasn't just one video. David urgently moved around the site to view other clips. All the same. Small edits, small insertions, tiny little alterations that no-one else would notice. Just in tune with his dialogue enough to fit into the spaces, or replace inanities, parts people were unlikely to miss. Exhorting action now, as well as thought. Nudging the lessons towards instruction, in exactly the way he'd feared.

David gulped heavily as the ramifications sank in. Whoever had done this knew exactly what they were doing. It was so deliberate, so precise. And the format… another hammer blow. As a part of his quest to remain unknown, the clips had been streamed over the internet. It hadn't been an issue at the time. Everyone had broadband now, and the streaming technology he'd used meant that the layman wouldn't be able to download or save the films, so they would have to log on to watch again, increasing the number of hits on the site in the process. Experts could find a way to download them of course, computers were never 100% securable, but the man in the street wouldn't have any of his clips saved. Which meant that even if someone was observant enough to think something was out of place, 99% of the time they'd have nothing to compare the new video with. He moved back to the most recent video clip that had been uploaded.

"As you can see, contrary to some reports I still have all my hair... and of course, I still have my convictions, and some pieces of advice for you, my children... and its time for me to stop holding you back... for <u>you</u> to stop holding back... and to stop those people who would hold us all back..."

The figure steepled his fingers, in that frequent mannerism of the Man in the Bath, and paused for effect. It could be re-used and re-edited footage with a new soundtrack, or superimposed on the original background, it didn't matter, as the end result was the same. To all intents and purposes, this was new, 'real,' Man in the Bath footage.

"... I can trust you all, in the 'Community,' to do the right thing, I know that now, but it's still difficult for one man alone to guide everyone... which is why I've allowed some other people from the Community, some who have been here since the beginning and who trust in me, to relay my message personally on my behalf... all for you, my friends..."

"Shit..."

The implications burrowed deeper and deeper, and three minutes later, he found himself bent over the toilet bowl, retching. In the background the voice drifted, thin and metallic from the small computer speakers.

"... it's time to think about human nature... now, some people are misguided and misinformed, they can't help that... but it is the duty of all right minded, enlightened people, to help guide these poor souls towards salvation... not all will want to, and that's fine... no-one should ever be coerced or forced... so long as they aren't causing problems..."

David retched again.

David put his right hand up to balance against the alley wall and coughed, feeling vomit rise to the back of his throat, and swallowing it down again.

The last rejection by Nadine had been the final straw. It had been weeks now, weeks that he'd been hiding away. Thinking. Planning. But before he made his final, risky, all-or-nothing attempt at redemption; first he'd known that he needed to speak to Nadine one more time, to try one last time. For some reason, she was the one he'd identified as the person he needed to admit everything to. Someone had to know the whole truth. One person had to believe him. Believe him, and forgive him.

David had even written it all down, spending days getting the words exactly right, just in case she didn't want to let him inside to listen. He'd planned for every eventuality. Even at best, he hadn't been hoping for anything other than a supportive shoulder from Nadine. That, and the presence of another human being to listen to him, but she hadn't even opened the door. Looking through the letterbox and shouting that she didn't want to see him, ever, and that she'd call the police if he approached her, and she'd accused him of terrible things. Hateful, untrue things.

David had just wanted her to know. He had wanted to give her what he'd written in person, to make sure that she read it, but with that option now impossible, he'd pushed the pages through the letterbox while she'd threatened him again with the police. In his mind, Nadine had been the rock to tie sanity around. The one person who'd always recognised what he was truly like, the mental games he played, that he wasn't a bad person. He forced the page through. It was part of the plan that she must as least have the opportunity to read it. At the back of his mind was the question of why it should be Nadine he was locking on to. Did she really know him better than anyone else?

It stayed at the back of his mind. The answer which he refused to admit, was that there was no-one else. Liz wouldn't answer, or even acknowledge his phone calls and e-mails. Since the day in the pub, Saint seemed to have vanished totally from existence. Even David's family refused to speak to him, or see him. Nadine had been the one hope. She'd forgiven him in the past, had always shared a bond with him. Deep down, she was his friend. But the venom he'd heard in her voice...

David looked down at his dishevelled clothes and it occurred, through the fug of the whisky, that maybe if he'd shaved and showered first, Nadine might have been slightly more receptive. After calling at her flat, he'd needed another drink, so had stumbled to The Royal Oak, and the memory of seeing himself in the mirror of the toilets made him feel slightly sick again. He'd looked as bad as he felt. Another two whiskies, and he'd been ushered out of the pub physically, staring at the faces who would have respected and admired him mere weeks before, but now who universally ignored him, pretended he wasn't there, or just gave disdainful looks. Shouting abuse at them probably hadn't helped, but by then David had been past caring.

That had been less than half an hour ago. David Dunn's final plan had been at the centre of his existence all evening and had moved inexorably closer to its conclusion in those last 30 minutes. Taking a deep gulp of the polluted air, he sniffed at the particles of burnt matter that were filling the sky, and staggered forwards. There was one just final chance for redemption. People had to believe him, and see him for who he really was. In the flesh. He knew what he had to do. This was where the Priest was due to be. Everyone had said. He could confront the imposter in plain sight, man to man.

It was ten minutes later that Dr David Dunn reached the back stragglers of the crowd, and heard the full roar of the assembled populace. He paused, leaning on the metal rail at the top of the steps, as he looked out over the panorama. And blinked in amazement.

There must have been twenty thousand people packed into the square and the surrounding streets. There were police officers in groups, dotted here and there, but they didn't seem concerned by the size or actions of the Community. Some even seemed to be chanting along with the rest of the crowd, and the whole scene had more of the atmosphere of a party than a danger, which was unexpected. David didn't notice the odd glances any more, nor the people shuffling away from his dishevelled, almost unrecognisable form.

At the far end of the grass, there was a large scaffold platform erected, covered with a billowing blue, yellow and red canopy, which bore an accurate and huge copy of his distinctive tattoo.

To the left and right of the stage were large bonfires, staffed by what appeared to be dozens of members of The Beatles, all in outfits from the cover of the Sergeant Pepper album. The crowd seemed to merge into queues on each side of the stage, and as he struggled to take it all in, David realised that when they reached the front, they were adding fuel to the bonfires which were providing the burning smell in his nostrils. He couldn't see what they were burning, but placards, papers and books seemed to be fanning the flames, and as he watched, several people stripped off all of their clothes to throw them onto the fire too, being greeted by huge cheers when they did so, apparently for the symbolism rather than the nudity. Whatever the symbolism was meant to convey.

He scanned back and forth, and picked out several more costumed people (other than The Beatles), scattered throughout the throng and he vaguely recognised prisoner suits, priests, and various other figures mentioned in his numerous narratives.

Large screens at the back of the stage were showing looped showreels of the webcam clips, or some of them anyway. Even from this distance, it was loud enough and large enough for him to recognise that several were completely new, and even the original ones being shown had changed, both in voice, and in the tone and editing. It made his bile rise once again.

In the centre of the stage was a large white screen, backlit to show the shadow of a figure in an oversized bath. A large neon clock over his head showed a countdown, currently at five minutes. David grunted and looked down as a piece of paper flapped against his feet. Struggling to keep balanced he picked the flyer up and strained his eyes to focus on the words revealing that the 'Man in the Bath' would personally address the rally live at exactly 8pm. David's watch swam into view, and his head swivelled up to the view below him, making the connection to the countdown clock with surprising alacrity. His eyes found the paper again and, squinting to concentrate, he grasped the general idea of the rest of the text. The 'Man in the Bath' would address his 'children' direct for the first time from the screen, pixelated live to retain his anonymity, and reveal what he wanted from them. The mysterious unveiling of 'The Purpose.' This explained the vast numbers and the camera crews he now spotted at various points through the people.

"Can't... can't let him..."

David squinted at the stage and saw the large line of heavily built figures across the front, holding anyone back with a physical decisiveness if they tried to get too close. He wasn't aware of the words falling helplessly from his own lips.

"Have... to try..."

The plan that had been developing over the previous weeks sprang up with renewed force. If the people saw him, heard him, in the flesh, then they'd have to know it was all fake, that they were being tricked. He staggered sideways, grabbing onto a heavily built man for support. This time they'd believe him. If they saw just him in the flesh.

"Hey there fella... careful... Jesus... you stink... you should show a bit more respect... showing up like that."

He was pushed away, and stumbled back against the rail.

"Hey, come on, leave him alone. There's room for everyone in the Community. He can't help being a tramp!"

The voice came from a well dressed woman with ridiculously coiffured hair, seated on a folding deckchair, along with several others.

"I'm just saying. It's disrespectful to Him! And if the priests see him, they won't be so gentle!"

David swayed and blinked hard. He'd forgotten about the 'priests.' They'd sprung up in the last month, devotees of the 'Community,' self-appointed to guide people. The website had done nothing to denounce them.

These priests were little more than thugs, dressed bizarrely in an assortment of bathrobes, and taking issue with any dissenting voices, via the medium of knives, and lumps of wood. Their appearance would have been amusing if not for those details. The fact that this group seemed to be loosely controlled by the Community, and only tended to target people who were on the fringes of society, or apparently causing trouble, had meant that they were allowed to continue their activities unhindered, and uncriticised. Even the police didn't publicly intervene. The priests were very careful that the damage they did never led to death. They were 'educators,' not murderers. That was the line anyway, and no-one had yet found a body.

David shook himself. It was ridiculous. It was totally insane. He straightened, and ran his hand through his short, greasy hair, clearing his throat as best he could.

"I... I'm not a tramp... I mean a homeless... person... I'm... Dr David... Dunn... and I'm here to tell you... I'm here to tell you..."

He turned carefully, cleared his throat, and shouted the line with as much authority as he could muster, drawing the attention of several people sitting on the steps below.

"I'm here to tell you that you've been deceived... you are being deceived right now..."

He took a deep breath, enunciating as clearly as he could, and hoping that the people wouldn't notice the slurring, which he was worryingly quite aware of, even in his drunken state. He knew he only had one chance here, and had to be very careful. Get their attention fast.

Licking his lips, David grabbed the front of his stained blue shirt and ripped the buttons open, causing more people to turn their heads, and some quiet laughter. Pulling the material off his right shoulder was more difficult than he'd imagined, and he stood there, side on, shirt halfway off and stretched across his chest, showing off his tattoo.

"He's fake! I'm the real 'Man in the Bath'... listen to me!"

More heads turned this time, and the instances of laughter increased too. David struggled to get the shirt off.

"It was me... I made the website... look... look at my tattoo..."

The man who'd pushed David away grunted.

"It's that prick off the telly... where are the priests?"

"Hey. Dickhead...... nice try mate!"

David turned to the new voice and saw a slim man with long hair, wrapped in a pony tail, standing halfway down the steps. With his t-shirt pulled off his right shoulder, he was showing a matching tattoo.

With an alarming wave of movement several other people bared their shoulders too. A young goth, a middle aged woman on a floral dress, a girl in a hooped green top, who could only just have been into her teens, all with exact replica of the previously unique tattoo design from the arm of Dr David Dunn. The ponytailed man laughed.

"I'm Spartacus!"

The ripples of laughter spread through the people, and Dave staggered back, trying to take in the scene.

"But listen to me... listen to my voice..."

Even to his own ears it sounded ridiculous, high pitched, and twisted by his alcohol-impaired lips.

"I'm had enough of this!"

A hand on his shoulder spun Dave round, and a fist hit him squarely on the nose. And then he was on his back on the cold concrete, the world spinning around him. His right hand slowly and gingerly lifted to his face, quite surprised to find it his nose unbroken. An angry male face glowered down at him.

"You can stay, but shut up... and stay out of trouble... this is important to some of us!"

His head lolling, Dr David Dunn took in the full glory of the panorama below the steps, panting for breath. From this angle, it truly was an amazing sight. So many people, so much laughter, so much gaiety. His eyes stopped on the stage, where there seemed to be a lot of movement, and focused on the countdown clock that was now passing the 59 seconds mark.

With difficulty, he hoisted himself to his feet once more, using the railings as support, and watched from the corner of his eye, where several people were peering suspiciously in his direction. David held his right hand up, as though in submission, and heard several mutterings. Then heard nothing clearly as a huge swell of noise worked its way upwards from the masses of the Community. They were counting down, as one voice, people punching the air and hollering as the numbers worked steadily lower.

"Twenty nine, twenty eight, twenty seven..."

A kind of helplessness swept over Dave Dunn, almost caught up in the wave of euphoria. Which was when the thought struck him.

This, all this, was the result of the actions and thoughts of Dr David Dunn. That it had been hijacked was secondary. There were thousands of people here. There were television crews from around the globe. All around the World, people were counting down too, waiting for the words of the 'Man in the Bath.' Pride and nausea mingled in him at the sight of it all, and the realisation he'd been the one to create this Frankenstein. And from no-where he felt the urge to giggle.

As the numbers dropped to single digits, the noise magically seemed to lower, the last five spoken at great volume, but in an eerie kind of whisper. And then silence. Total, deafening silence as every eye in the crowd turned towards the stage and waited.

And he couldn't help it. He started to giggle out loud. A few eyes swivelled his way, about to object but before they could move, he took a deep breath and bellowed at the top of his lungs:

"I'M SPARTACUS!"

Chp 29 – Sounds of Silence

The last thing Dr David Dunn ever saw, was a blur of light brown movement, followed by a few moments of bright blackness, interspersed with firework-like circles of a vivid scarlet colour.

The last thing his ears heard, was the soft wind-like swooshing sound of the lump of wood swinging through the air, originating from above his left temple.

The last thought that passed through his intact skull, was that this was possibly the most beautiful sound he'd ever heard in his life. And that he was surprised he'd never heard it before.

To all my viewers, supporters, and subscribers. This website is closing. It's now served its purpose. Thank you for all your support over the time I've been posting.

I know a lot of you still want to know who I am, but the fact of the matter is, I'm not important as a person. It's the idea of 'The Man in the Bath' that was important, and that will live on, even without this website. If you think you need to know my actual name, then you're missing the point.

When I started, I just wanted to throw out my ideas, and hope that some other people would share theirs too. What I've said isn't really important in the big scheme of things. What matters is what you think about our World, and what you do with that knowledge. Whether you choose to use it for good, or for ill.

Who was I? I was the man sat at the next table who you didn't debate with, who may have been able to tell you important things. I was the child who used to ask questions, and then stopped asking out loud with age. I used to be the silent majority, until I found my voice. I'm the little voice that objects to the things you know are wrong. And I'm just a guy in the tub, telling tales.

I was the Man in the Bath
My final message to you, my gift, to those few who want it ...

My cup overfloweth. Thrice.

<u>www.ManintheBath.com/home.html</u>

This page is now unavailable. It could be a problem with your service provider or a problem with your settings.

Please contact your system administrator.

Contact me

Thank you for reading *Man in the Bath.*

If you enjoyed my writing, why not log onto www.kitderrick.com and sign up for the newsletter, to be notified when I publish something new.

Alternatively, follow me at the tweetyplace on @kitderrick1

Also available by the same author:

tEXt me: A Brief Encounter With A Nokia 3310
The Raven Sound
Hope Is A Six Letter Word

www.ingramcontent.com/pod-product-compliance
Lightning Source LLC
Chambersburg PA
CBHW051503030726
47592CB00006B/2076